SPECTRE COLLECTORS

A NEW YORK NIGHTMARE!

BARRY HUTCHISON

nosy crow

First published 2018 by Nosy Crow Ltd
The Crow's Nest, 14 Baden Place, Crosby Row
London SE1 1YW, UK
www.nosycrow.com

ISBN: 978 1 78800 039 0

Nosy Crow and associated logos are trademarks
and/or registered trademarks of Nosy Crow Ltd

Text © Barry Hutchison, 2018
Cover and inside illustrations Rob Biddulph, 2018

The right of Barry Hutchison and Rob Biddulph to be identified as the
author and illustrator respectively has been asserted.

A CIP catalogue record for this book is available from the British Library.

Printed and bound in the UK by Clays Ltd, Elcograf S.p.A.
Typeset by Tiger Media

Papers used by Nosy Crow are made from wood grown in
sustainable forests.

1 3 5 7 9 8 6 4 2

For Tommy Donbavand,
the toughest guy in all
of Tough Town.

B. H.

CHAPTER 1

Denzel Edgar was halfway through the Hall of Mirrors when he saw the ghost.

It was standing in front of a short, squat mirror, jumping up and down and flapping its arms at its sides like a chicken.

"Here, Denzel, check this out. What do I look like?" said Smithy. "I'll give you a clue. Bu-buuck!"

Smithy was small, scrawny and generally a bit untidy. Those were the first things people noticed about him. What most people didn't notice was that he'd been dead for the better part of five hundred years. Even Denzel had only discovered this fact quite recently, despite having been best mates with him for ages.

"Shh. Shut up," Denzel whispered. He turned slowly, the beam of his torch reflecting strangely across the peeling walls and bare wooden floor. "We're supposed to be looking for the ... thing. The whatchamacallit?"

"Ghost?" said Smithy.

"Yes, but ... Boyle called it something. It had a proper name."

"Gavin?" Smithy guessed.

Denzel shone the torch in Smithy's face, but Smithy didn't flinch. "What? No! I mean like an official scientific name. Free-formed Vaporous... Oh, I don't know."

He looked down at the garish ring on his finger. The gemstone was supposed to light up when anything supernatural was nearby, but it was currently dark. That should have been comforting, but as Denzel knew for a fact there was at least one ghost in the room – currently strutting back and forth, pretending to be a flightless bird – the lifeless gem didn't fill him with confidence.

The walkie-talkie on Denzel's belt crackled into life, making him jump. He fumbled for the radio, almost dropped his torch, then briefly juggled them both for a few frantic seconds, as the voice of a gruff teenager spat from the tinny speaker.

"Denzel. Anything? Over."

2

SPECTRE COLLECTORS

Denzel managed to stop juggling and found the "talk" button on the side of the radio's plastic casing. "Uh. No. There's just a load of mirrors."

He released the button and waited for a reply. When none came, he *thonked* himself on the side of the head with the torch and pressed the button again. "Sorry. Over. Sorry, Boyle. I mean ... over."

"Keep looking," said Boyle. "We're definitely picking up Spectral Energy. What's Smithy doing? Over."

Denzel pressed the button and glanced over to where Smithy was checking himself out in another mirror. "Right now? A handstand," said Denzel. "Over."

"Ha! Think you can turn me upside down, do you? Not so clever now!" Smithy told the mirror, then he lost his balance and crashed, feet first, into it. The mirror fell in a din of smashing glass and Smithy sprang upright like a startled gazelle.

"What was that? Over," Boyle demanded.

Denzel hesitated with his finger over the button. "Uh, nothing," he said. "False alarm. Thought it was a ghost, but it wasn't."

"It was a *goat*," said Smithy, leaning over to speak into the walkie-talkie. He winked at Denzel and gave him a thumbs-up.

Denzel mouthed at him to be quiet, then laughed

falsely. "Haha. Not really. That would be ... mad. But we're OK here. Nothing to report, over."

There was a lengthy pause from the other end, then: "Keep your eyes peeled. And if you see something, do *not* engage. Over and out."

"Uh. OK. Bye," Denzel said into the radio, then he clipped it back on to his belt.

Smithy waggled his eyebrows and grinned goofily. "I think he fell for the goat thing."

Denzel sighed. It had been a week since he and Smithy had officially been made members of the Spectre Collectors – a top-secret organisation dedicated to protecting the world from supernatural threats – and neither of them was exactly getting the hang of it.

"It's not really fair, is it?" he said.

"What's not fair?"

"Well, I mean ... Boyle and Samara are teamed up together. She can do magic; he's got, like, all the guns in the world."

Smithy frowned. "So?"

"So what have we got? A couple of torches, a walkie-talkie and a ring that's cutting the circulation off in my finger."

Smithy slipped an arm around Denzel's shoulder and began to sing quietly in his ear while swaying from side to side. "You and me, we got each other, just a couple of pals in a creepy old circus."

Denzel shrugged him away. "Get off," he said, but he couldn't stop himself smiling. "Anyway, it's not a circus, it's a creepy old *fairground*."

"Is it? What's the difference?" Smithy asked.

"Well, lots of things," said Denzel. "You don't get animals at a fairground."

"There's animals here," said Smithy. "Look."

He pointed his torch into one of the corners. The light reflected off a tiny pair of eyes. "See?"

"That's a rat," said Denzel, fighting the urge to run away screaming. "They don't count."

They pressed on through the Hall of Mirrors, catching misshapen reflections of themselves leering out of every rotten frame.

"That's a point," Denzel said, keeping his distance from the corner with the rat in it. "Can you get ghost animals?"

"Oh yeah, definitely," said Smithy. "You can get ghost anything. Even inanimate objects. I saw a ghost lizard once."

Denzel shot him a sideways glance. "A ghost lizard?"

"Yep. A *chamelo*, or something. It was in a pet shop. This kid touched it then – *pchow* – it disappeared."

"Could it maybe have been a chamel*eon*?"

Smithy clicked his fingers. "That was it! Pchow," he said, waving his fingers mysteriously in front of Denzel's face and whispering. "Disappeared."

"You've literally just described all chameleons."

"What? *All* chameleons are ghosts?"

"No," said Denzel, then he decided it wasn't worth the effort. "Forget it. Yeah, that is some spooky stuff, all right."

"Oh, and I also saw someone get eaten by a ghost lion once," said Smithy. He tapped himself on the side of the head. "But I've pretty much blocked that memory out. Onwards!"

He marched off towards the door at the far end of the hall, leaving Denzel to try to figure out if he was joking or not. It was hard to tell with Smithy. Denzel sometimes wondered if even Smithy himself knew, half the time.

They stepped out of the Hall of Mirrors and into the cool night breeze. Empty popcorn tubs fluttered across the overgrown grass like disappointing butterflies, their colourful print long since faded. The rusted metal of an old roller coaster creaked and groaned as the wind whistled between its legs and through its crumbling tracks.

"What about clowns?" asked Smithy.

"What about them?"

"Are they circuses or fairgrounds?"

"Circuses," said Denzel.

"Good. I hate clowns," said Smithy. "Oh! Here's one. What would you rather – be trapped in a cage with a killer clown..."

"Right."

"Or be trapped in a cage with a bear?"

"Well—"

"*But*," continued Smithy, who wasn't finished. "The bear is dressed like a clown, and the clown is dressed like a bear."

Denzel frowned. "Who's dressing bears up like clowns?"

Smithy shrugged. "I don't know. The government."

They set off towards the next building on the list Boyle had given them of places to check. Boyle himself would be over by the big wheel with Samara, which was where the actual ghost-sighting had taken place. Denzel reckoned he and Smithy had been sent to scope out the other places mainly to keep them out of the way.

"So let me get this straight. The government has dressed a bear up like a clown..."

"And a clown up like a bear," Smithy added.

"Right. And a clown up like a bear, and – for reasons

unknown – is making me choose which one I want to be put in a cage with," said Denzel. "And no matter which one I pick, they're going to try to kill me."

"Exactamundo," said Smithy. "So which do you choose?"

Denzel kicked a decomposing soft toy that was tangled in the grass. Its head came off, spraying damp stuffing across the ground. "Clown dressed like a bear, probably," he said.

"Interesting. How come?"

"Well, if I was a bear and someone dressed me like a clown, I'd be *furious*," Denzel reasoned. "I wouldn't stand a chance fighting that; it'd rip me to bits. But a clown in a bear suit is going to be quite clumsy, I reckon. If he's got a big headpiece on, it'd make it hard for him to see, wouldn't it? I could just push him over."

Smithy nodded slowly. "OK. What if the bear was invisible and the clown could fly?"

"Shh," Denzel hissed. "Did you hear that?"

"Yes. You did it right in my ear," said Smithy.

"No, not me going 'shh'. That noise."

They both listened. The only sounds were the creaking and groaning of the fairground around them.

"I don't hear anything," said Smithy. "What sort of noise was it?"

"I don't know," said Denzel. "It was sort of a…"

"*Ptwing?*" Smithy guessed.

"No, like…"

"*Barudda-dudda-dudda?*"

"What is that supposed to be?" asked Denzel.

"What, 'Barudda-dudda-dudda'? Just a noise," said Smithy. "Why, was it like that?"

"No, it was more…"

A low moan drifted through the open archway of the building ahead of them, making all the hairs on Denzel's neck stand on end.

"Like that," he whispered.

The archway had been painted to look like a gaping mouth. Two red eyes leered out over the top of the arch, and above those, in faded lettering, were two little words that sent a chill tickling down Denzel's spine.

Ghost Train.

CHAPTER 2

Denzel held the walkie-talkie to his mouth and whispered into the microphone.

"Hey, Boyle. I think we might have found something. Over."

There was a hiss of static from the other side, then an enormous severed head appeared floating in the air in front of him. Denzel and Smithy both grabbed each other and screamed in fright.

"Hey, guys!" Samara said, her semi-transparent giant face breaking into a smile.

Denzel groaned with a mixture of embarrassment and relief. He quickly released his grip on Smithy and brushed down the front of his black jumper. "Samara. You, uh, you startled us," said Denzel.

"Really? Didn't notice," said Samara, clearly fighting the urge to laugh. "Anyway, Boyle's a little busy at the moment."

"Cool! Is he fighting a ghost?" asked Smithy, keen to hear every exciting detail.

"Uh, no. He stood on dog poo," said Samara.

"Oh, well, thanks a lot for telling them," said Boyle from somewhere in the background.

"What have you found?" Samara asked.

"Denzel heard a noise," said Smithy.

Samara's floating face frowned. "What sort of noise?"

"That's what I asked," said Smithy. "At first, I wondered if it was a sort of 'ptwing'-type noise, but he said—"

The moaning came again, echoing from the darkened tunnel of the Ghost Train.

"It was like that," said Denzel.

Samara shrugged. At least, Denzel guessed that's why her head bobbed about the way it did, but as she had no visible shoulders it was difficult to be sure. "That? That's nothing. Just the wind. Check it out though. No harm in having a look."

"Unless it's something horrible that kills us," Smithy pointed out.

"Yeah," agreed Samara. "But I'm, like, ninety per cent sure it won't be."

Another moan rang out. "Well, maybe eighty-five."

"Oh, come on, not again! Seriously, why can't people just pick it up?" Boyle cried. Samara's floating head turned, as if looking back over one of her missing shoulders. "I'd better go. Keep us posted."

The head popped like a bubble. Denzel puffed out his cheeks. "Well, that was reassuring."

Smithy peered into the tunnel. It was like gazing down the throat of a giant dragon. The flaking paintwork made the monstrous face look even worse, as if it had a terrible contagious skin condition just waiting to be passed on.

"Should we go in then?" he asked.

"We could," said Denzel. "Or we could just wait out here and pretend we did."

Smithy nodded slowly. "What would you rather, right? Go in there, or have Samara and Boyle find out you're a big chicken?"

Denzel weighed the two options up. It didn't take long. Creepy dark tunnel or not, there was no contest really.

"Fine," he said, striding towards the gaping maw of the Ghost Train. "But if I get horribly killed, you're *totally* getting haunted."

Denzel's torchlight cut a thin line through the darkness as he shuffled along the Ghost Train's tracks. Smithy stuck close behind him, jumping at every creak of the rotten floor.

"You're pretty nervous for someone who's already dead," Denzel whispered.

"No I'm not," Smithy protested. "I'm just ... guarding the rear."

"Right," said Denzel. He glanced down to his shoulder, where Smithy's hand was gripping his jumper. "It's just you seem to be using me as a human shield."

"Well, can you blame me?" Smithy whispered. "Look at this place!"

He swept his own torch across the wooden walls. It picked out six severed heads, two big spiders and a plastic skeleton with an arm missing.

"This is the worst place in the world!" Smithy hissed.

Strangely enough, now they were inside, Denzel was far less scared than he'd been when they were standing outside. It was the plastic skeleton that had done it. It had reminded him of every other Ghost Train he'd ever been on, where the shocks were boring, the effects were naff and the scariest part of the whole thing was the ticket price.

"It's all fake, relax," said Denzel. "Samara was right.

There's nothing to worry about."

"Oh?" Smithy squeaked. "Then why's your finger glowing?"

Denzel raised his hand. The ring on his finger pulsed an ominous shade of purple.

A cold breeze drifted along the dark passageway, and Denzel's breath became a series of fluffy purple-tinged clouds.

Denzel swallowed and tightened his grip on his torch. "It's still probably nothing," he said, although he wasn't sure who he was trying to convince. "The ring must just be picking you up."

"It hasn't picked me up before," Smithy pointed out.

"Yeah, but you haven't been holding on to me and crying before."

"I'm not crying," Smithy protested. "Not yet, anyway. But I'm not ruling it out."

"Let's keep going," Denzel said. "We can't be far from the end."

A deep, rumbling moan vibrated the walls of the tunnel, making the plastic skeleton flap and jangle around.

"Or we could turn around and run as fast as we can," Denzel squeaked. "I'm happy either way."

The moan rose in pitch, becoming an ear-splitting

screech, like claws being dragged down a blackboard. Denzel and Smithy exchanged a glance, both nodded at the same time, then spun on the spot and plunged back the way they'd come.

A few paces in, they were met by a low, guttural growl. A bright white light began to strobe, revealing the silhouette of something large, hairy and eye-wateringly terrifying. The ring on Denzel's finger blazed red, reflecting off the monster's grey head – the only part of its body not covered in coarse hair – and its dozens of shark-like teeth.

Denzel made a noise. It wasn't a noise he was particularly proud of – a sort of yelping "Bleaurmwa!" that rose from his toes – but it burst from his mouth all on its own, and he felt that, given the circumstances, it was perfectly understandable.

"This way!" cried Smithy.

Denzel was pulled towards the closest wall. He threw up his hands to protect himself, but then passed right through the wood and stumbled into another corridor on the other side.

"Nice ghost skills," he panted.

"Thanks," said Smithy. "What was that thing?"

"I don't know!" said Denzel. "Some kind of, like, shark-headed ... monkey thing."

Smithy wrinkled his nose. "Monkey? You think? I'd have said bear."

Denzel flashed his torch across the walls. They were in a different part of the ride now. A filthy old sheet dangled from the ceiling, three black circles representing its ghostly face. An old cuckoo clock hung on one wall, a little rubber bat dangling limply from the open doors.

"I could be wrong," said Smithy. "But I reckon we're still in the Ghost Train."

"Oh, you think?" whispered Denzel.

His torch flickered and he had to thump the side a few times to steady the beam. Mind you, even without the torch, the light from Denzel's ring was more than bright enough to see by. It shone with a blazing swirl of oranges and reds that danced across the walls like sunlight reflecting off rippling water.

Another sound hissed along the passageway towards them. Denzel held his breath. "Did you hear that?"

"What now?" Smithy croaked.

"Sort of a ... whooshing. Like a lot of people whispering or—"

"A million tiny wings all flapping at the same time?" said Smithy.

"Yeah," said Denzel. "Yeah, I suppose it..."

He saw Smithy illuminated by the ring's glow. He

stood with his back to Denzel, pointing along the tunnel. Denzel raised his torch just as hundreds of black bats flooded the passageway, chittering and screeching as they battered off the walls and bounced against the ceiling.

"Run!" Denzel cried, turning and racing the other way. Smithy clattered along behind him as the first of the bats came *whistling* past, leathery wings frantically beating the air.

Denzel's torch flickered again. He stumbled on, slamming it against his hip, trying to hammer it back into life.

BAM! He collided with something, face-first, and staggered backwards. The glow from the ring illuminated a green-skinned zombie standing directly in front of him. Denzel had his mouth all the way open and a scream racing halfway up his windpipe before he realised the zombie was painted on to a wall.

"Here they come!" yelped Smithy, barrelling along the tunnel. Behind him, the darkness heaved with the vast cloud of bats.

"Dead end!" Denzel howled.

"Not for long!" cried Smithy, throwing himself into a rugby tackle and slamming his shoulder into Denzel's stomach.

Denzel *oofed* as all the air was knocked out of him, then he flew backwards through the wall, stumbled over a ledge on the other side and fell with a *thump* on to another set of tracks.

Smithy rolled off him and they both lay on the rotten tracks, catching their breath. At least, Denzel caught his breath. Smithy hadn't breathed in years.

"Oh, man," Denzel wheezed. "That was close. Nice save."

"Thanks," said Smithy. He raised his head, looked around, then let it flop back down again. "I think we're safe here."

Denzel's ring let out a high-pitched *whine* as the red glow grew brighter and more vibrant. There was a *bang* as the ring exploded and darkness rushed in around them.

A moment later, the darkness was pierced by a single white light shining along the tracks. A whistle echoed down the line.

CHOO-CHOOOOO!

Smithy glanced across to Denzel and smiled nervously. "Although 'safe' might be a bit of an exaggeration."

CHAPTER 3

Smithy and Denzel were both screaming when they tumbled through the final wall of the Ghost Train. They stumbled on for a few desperate paces, then collapsed in a trembling heap on the ground.

"Are ... are we alive?" Smith asked.

"I am," wheezed Denzel, although his voice was muffled thanks to Smithy having landed on top of him. "Pretty sure you're still dead."

"Say cheese!"

Denzel's face was mostly covered by Smithy's butt. He wriggled free in time for a bright-white flash to go off in his face.

"Hey!" he protested.

"Oh, man, that is *so* going on the notice board," said Boyle, looking at the screen of his camera. He showed Samara and they both grinned.

"Oh, yeah. That's getting blown up," Samara agreed. "Poster size."

Denzel and Smithy clambered to their feet. "What? No! What are you...?" Denzel shook his head. "There's no time to muck around," he told them, pointing back in the direction of the Ghost Train. "That place is, like, ghost central."

"He's right. It's *hoaching* in there!" agreed Smithy. We saw this shark—"

"Bear—"

"*Monkey* thing!" Denzel finished. "With big teeth and claws, and—"

"Bats!" Smithy yelped, his whole body convulsing. "Lots of bats!"

Denzel nodded. "Lots of bats! So many bats! And ... and..."

His voice trailed off when he saw the expressions on Boyle and Samara's faces. "What?" he asked. "What's so funny?"

"Hmm?" Samara squeaked, pinching the side of her mouth between finger and thumb. "Hmm? Funny?

No, nothing."

"Nothing," agreed Boyle, but then both Spectre Collectors erupted into howls of laughter. "Oh, man. Their faces," said Boyle, his reddening face clashing with the blue and silver camouflage of his Vulteron uniform.

Samara wiped her eyes on the hem of her Oberon cloak. "Oh, that was beautiful. I'm sorry, guys," she said, but the way she gasped and snorted suggested she wasn't actually *that* sorry at all. "You see, well, the thing is... We set you up."

Denzel and Smithy exchanged a glance. "What do you mean?" demanded Denzel.

"We do this with all new recruits," Boyle wheezed. "Not just us, I mean. Everyone."

"It's Spectre Collectors tradition, really. We went through it too," Samara said, trying – without much success – to bring her hysterics under control. "Think of it as your initiation ceremony."

Smithy sniffed and nodded. "Yep. Yep, that's what I thought. I didn't believe it for a second."

Denzel frowned. "Oh yeah? Then why were you screaming?"

"I wasn't screaming," said Smithy. He shifted uncomfortably. "I was ... communicating with dolphins."

Denzel held up his hand, showing the black soot-mark

where the ring had been. "What about the ring? You said it detected Spectral Energy."

Boyle held up a little remote control, no bigger than his thumb. He clicked a series of buttons on the front. "Purple. Red. Boom!"

"That's just ... *mean*," said Denzel. He jabbed a thumb back in the direction of the Ghost Train again. "So ... all of that was fake? The monster? The bats?"

Boyle grinned. It was possibly the first time Denzel had ever seen the older boy smile. It didn't suit him. "Yup!"

"The train?"

Samara's smile flickered, just a fraction. "The what?" she asked, but before Denzel could answer, an ancient old steam locomotive exploded through the wall behind him.

Smithy covered his head with his hands, dropped to his knees and began loudly communicating with dolphins again. The train bore down on them, its headlight blazing in the late-evening gloom, sulphurous green smoke billowing from its chimney.

CHOOOOOOOO!

Denzel froze, his hands raised in front of his face, his eyes tightly shut as the train hurtled directly towards him.

And then, with a *crackle* from Boyle's assault rifle,

22

the train exploded. Denzel ducked and a tidal wave of ectoplasmic goo hurtled over his head. He heard a loud, wet *KERSPLAT*, then Samara and Boyle both yelped in shock.

When Denzel and Smithy straightened up, they saw the two Spectre Collectors standing in a slowly expanding puddle of gloop, their faces a picture of surprised horror. They stood with their arms at their sides, their legs slightly apart, and were covered from head to toe in what looked like the contents of a particularly violent sneeze. It plastered their hair to their heads and dribbled down their faces, before dripping into the puddle at their feet.

"N-no," said Samara, waddling uncomfortably on the spot. "The train? That's a new one on us."

"What, that's *never* happened before?" said Denzel. "Then why did it happen to us?"

"I don't think it did happen to you," said Boyle, scooping goo from his face. "I think it happened to *you*."

Smithy and Denzel exchanged puzzled looks. "You think it happened to *us* but not to *us*?" Denzel asked. "In what world does that make sense?"

"No!" Boyle snapped. "I mean it didn't happen to both of you. I think it was drawn to you, Denzel, specifically."

"You really should have made that clearer," Smithy said. "It was quite confusing."

"And why would it be drawn to me?" Denzel wondered.

"Why can you see poltergeists?" Boyle asked.

"I don't know," Denzel said.

"Nor do I," Boyle replied. He blew a wad of ectoplasm from one nostril. It landed on the ground with a *splut*. "But I'm going to find out."

A Vulteron girl with a big sneer and a bigger gun eyed Samara and Boyle as they shuffled from the elevator, ectoplasm *squelching* from their boots with every step.

Knightley had been waiting for Denzel and Smithy the first time they'd ever descended the lift into the Spectre Collectors' HQ. Unlike then, this time she didn't stick her gun in their faces and scream at them to get on the floor, but she did wear an expression that suggested she'd quite like to.

Denzel wasn't exactly sure why Knightley hated him so much. He had some ideas, mainly because she'd shouted them at him over the past few days. He didn't belong, he shouldn't be there, he didn't have what it took to be a Spectre Collector – that sort of thing.

Luckily for Denzel, she disliked Smithy even more, and regularly complained that having a ghost as part of the world's premier ghost-hunting organisation made a complete mockery of it. Fortunately, not many others seemed to share her opinion.

"What happened to you two?" Knightley snorted, looking Boyle and Samara up and down.

"Ghost Train," muttered Boyle through his clenched jaw.

"Oh yeah. Initiation," said Knightley, shooting Denzel and Smithy just the briefest of glances. Even in that fraction of a second, though, she managed to convey her disapproval. "That still doesn't explain why you're gunked."

"No, he means it was an *actual* Ghost Train," said Samara. "It came after Denzel. Boyle shot it and…" She gestured down at herself. "Ta-daa!"

Knightley frowned. "Since when was the fairground actually haunted? We've never picked up any activity there before, and we've been using that place for initiation since forever."

"Don't know. Right now, don't care," Boyle growled. "Send a squad to check it out. Right now, I just need a shower."

Knightley stepped aside. "OK. While you're doing that, Denzel will be packing his bags."

Denzel's eyes widened. "You're kicking me out?"

"Ugh. I wish," Knightley grunted. "You're going to New York."

"What, like, in America?"

Knightley tutted. "No, the *other* New York. Of course in America."

"But why?" asked Denzel. "What's in New York?"

"Loads of stuff," said Smithy. "Buildings. Cars. A zoo, probably." He gasped with excitement and turned to Knightley. "Is there a zoo?"

"The Cult of Sh'grath has an outpost there," Knightley explained, blanking Smithy completely.

Denzel and Smithy exchanged a glance. "Who's the Cult of Sh'grath."

Knightley squeezed the bridge of her nose between finger and thumb and muttered below her breath. "We are," she said. "The Cult of Sh'grath, the Messengers of the Allwhere, the Seventh Army of the Enlightened." She threw up her hands in despair and turned to Samara and Boyle. "Seriously, have you taught them anything? Anything at all?"

"I don't get it," said Denzel. "Why would New York want to see me?"

Knightley shrugged. "Because you're a freak," she said. "Because for centuries the Spectre Collectors has been made up of Vulterons, like me and Boyle, and Oberons like *her*" – she snapped her head in Samara's direction – "and then you come along and you don't fit anywhere."

She shot a glare in Smithy's direction. If the way she looked at Denzel was bad, the way she scowled at Smithy was even worse. "So I guess that's why they want to see you. Both of you. Frankly, if it means you're out of our hair, I'm all in favour."

"We could play baseball," said Smithy. He swung an imaginary baseball bat. "Batter up!"

"You're not going on holiday," Knightley told them. "Besides, if they've got any sense over there, they'll stick you in a cage and poke you with sticks."

"Still, it'll be a nice change, won't it?" said Smithy, without even a hint of sarcasm. "I've never been to America."

"Nor me," said Denzel.

The thought of it excited him. He'd seen New York hundreds of times in movies and on TV, and now he was going to see it in person. After the whole Ghost Train fiasco, the day – late as it now was – was shaping up to be pretty good, after all.

"How are we getting there?" he asked. "One of those magic shortcut tunnels you use? Do they hurt?"

"No, they don't, and no, you won't be. All tech- or magic-based transportation is short range only," said Samara. She had kicked off her boots and was removing her slime-soaked socks. "We use … another method for travelling long distances."

Denzel looked across the faces of the three Spectre Collectors. "Oh?" he said. "And what might that be?"

"I bet it's a big bubble thing," said Smithy. "Or, like, a flying horse. Or a jetpack. Or—"

"None of those," said Knightley, cutting him short. She smiled. It was not a kind smile. It wasn't even a particularly happy one. But it was a smile, all the same. "But trust me," she said. "You're going to love it."

CHAPTER 4

Denzel wriggled in his seat, trying in vain to get comfortable. The space between his chair and the one in front was ridiculously small, and the ridges of the plastic tray fixed to the other seat's back were digging into his knees.

"This is nice, isn't it?" said Smithy. He reached up and twisted a little dial on the ceiling panel above Denzel's head. A blast of icy-cold air hit Denzel in the face.

"Not really," Denzel said, switching the air off again. He fumbled with his seat belt. "How do you get this to clip together? It keeps coming apart."

"Dunno. I didn't bother," said Smithy, taking a tatty

and worn in-flight magazine from the seat pocket in front, and flicking through its torn pages. "I figure if we crash, it probably won't do me a lot of harm."

Across the aisle on Smithy's left, a young girl burst into tears. Smithy and Denzel both looked over to find the girl's mother glaring back. "Can you *please* not say that word?" she spat.

Smithy frowned. "What word?"

"*That* word. The word you just said," the woman continued. "You've upset my daughter."

"What, 'figure'?" Smithy guessed.

"No!"

"'Me'? 'Lot'? 'Probably'?"

"No!" hissed the woman.

"'It'? Surely not 'it'," said Smithy. "I won't get very far not saying 'it'."

"Crash!" the woman snapped. "OK? Don't say 'crash'!"

Beside her, her daughter's screaming became louder and more hysterical. "Now look what you've done," said the girl's mother, then she busied herself trying to distract the girl with a colouring book.

Denzel wriggled in his seat again, had a frantic moment when he wondered if he still had the passports, then relaxed when he found them in his inside pocket.

When Knightley had told them they'd be flying to New

York, Denzel had been quick to point out that he didn't have a passport, and Smithy – being dead – didn't have one either.

To his surprise, Knightley had produced documents for each of them, along with plane tickets for them to fly to New York in "Economy E Class". Once they'd arrived at the airport check-in desk, Denzel asked what the "E" was for, and was told it stood for "Economy".

He and Smithy had laughed about flying "Economy Economy Class", convinced it couldn't possibly be as bad as it sounded.

They were wrong.

"Here's one for you," said Smithy. "What would you rather, right? Spend the next six hours on this plane...?"

"Or?"

"Or be impaled on a big spike?"

It said a lot for the plane that Denzel had to give the question some serious thought. He already felt like his body was being permanently bent out of shape, and they hadn't even taken off yet.

Still, at least the seat on his right was empty. It was the one closest to the window, which meant he'd get a pretty decent view once they were in the air. It also gave him a bit of desperately needed extra leg room.

He turned to Smithy and was about to deliver his

answer when an enormously overweight man with a bright-red face shambled to a stop beside Smithy's seat. The man gasped and wheezed as he tried to get his breath back, before wiping the sweat from his forehead with a spotted handkerchief.

"Excuse me, lads," he panted, nodding to the empty seat beside Denzel. "I think that's mine."

Denzel looked at the enormous man. He looked at the little seat beside him. "Out of interest," he said, turning to Smithy. "Just how big a spike are we talking?"

Denzel descended the escalator, his suitcase upright on the step beside him. Smithy stood behind him, clinging to the handrail with both hands, and whimpering quietly. They were approaching the bottom, and the airport exit was just a short walk away.

Picking up his suitcase, Denzel stepped smoothly on to solid ground. He walked on a few paces, then turned in time to see Smithy leap awkwardly from the bottom step, do a sort of half-splits, then stagger forwards and fall flat on his face.

Smithy leapt to his feet immediately. "Meant that, totally meant that," he announced to the crowd of other escalator riders building up behind him, then he pulled the handle up on his case and wheeled it over to where

Denzel was waiting.

"Smooth," Denzel said.

"Moving stairs. It's not right," said Smithy. He looked around. Several people in suits stood around the bottom of the escalator, holding up cards with names on the front. "Isn't there supposed to be someone here to collect us?"

"Yeah, supposed to be," said Denzel, scanning the cards. He didn't find his or Smithy's name anywhere. He dug in his inside pocket until he found the notes Knightley had given him. "Someone called ... Weinberg."

"Could that be him?" Smithy asked, pointing to a man on the escalator.

"No, that's the guy who was sitting next to us on the plane," said Denzel. "For six hours."

Smithy nodded. "I thought I recognised him." He waved enthusiastically but the man just glared at him as he waddled past. "He doesn't look happy, does he?"

"No," Denzel agreed.

"Probably still angry at you for spilling your drink on him."

Denzel sighed. "That was you. You spilled your drink on him."

Smithy considered this. "Oh yeah. Yeah, so it was."

"Come on," said Denzel, pulling his case behind him.

"We'll go outside. Maybe this Weinberg guy is waiting out there."

They headed for the doors but the airport crowds made progress difficult. Everyone seemed to be in a rush as they bustled past, lost in their own little worlds, their cases clipping the ankles of everyone else around them.

"Excuse us," said Denzel. "Sorry. Coming through."

Denzel was navigating a path between a group of nuns and a gaggle of well-dressed businessmen all yakking into phones when he heard a voice whisper in his ear.

Go left.

"What?" Denzel said, turning to Smithy.

Smithy blinked. "What?"

"Did you just tell me to go left?"

"When?"

"A second ago."

Smithy thought back. "I don't think so. Why'd you ask?"

Denzel listened for a moment, then shrugged and continued towards the door. Three paces on, the voice came again.

Go left.

There was a door over in that direction. It wasn't an exit like the big sweeping glass doors up ahead, but a small, unassuming wooden door, with a small, unassuming metal sign on the front marked *Staff Only*.

Denzel waited for a break in the foot traffic, then cut across the flow. "Come on, I think we should go this way," he said, beckoning with his head for Smithy to follow.

The going was easier once they left the crowd behind. Denzel glanced back nervously, worried one of the scary American security guards was going to come racing after them, gun drawn. No one seemed to be paying them any attention though, and they made it all the way to the door without being apprehended or shot.

Through there, the voice whispered. It echoed slightly, as if Denzel's ear was at one end of a long pipe and the speaker was standing at the opposite end.

Glancing around again, Denzel tried the handle. It rattled but the door didn't budge. There was a keypad fixed to the wall beside the door, four little lines indicating where a PIN should go.

Denzel looked the door up and down. "It's locked," he announced.

Smithy let out a loud "Ha!" that came dangerously close to catching the attention of everyone else in the airport terminal. With a *shh* from Denzel, he lowered his voice to a whisper. "No door can keep us out, thanks to my incredible, amazing and..."

Smithy's voice tailed off. He watched as four digits

flashed up on the keypad. With a *clunk*, the door unlatched and swung open a few centimetres. A warm wind wafted out through the gap.

"Did you do that?" Smithy asked.

Denzel shook his head. "Wasn't me."

Inside, whispered the voice. *Hurry.*

"It says we should go in," said Denzel.

"What does?"

"The voice in my head."

Smithy stared at Denzel blankly for a few seconds, then shrugged. "Fair enough. If you can't trust a voice inside your own head, then who *can* you trust?" he said.

He nudged the door open.

They stepped into the shadowy room.

Then the floor gave way beneath them and they fell, screaming, into the dark.

CHAPTER 5

The darkness flickered, then Denzel blinked in a sudden bright whiteness that made his eyeballs ache. He was still falling, but now wind whistled around him, and the expanse of whiteness was drawing closer and closer. He could see his shadow on it now, with Smithy's beside it.

Several seconds of screaming later, Denzel hit the floor in a cramped, dimly-lit room. Clouds, he realised.

The white things were clouds.

He twisted his head around and looked up. Yep, there was the sky. Those were definitely clouds down below.

"Aaaaaaaaaargh!" Denzel screamed, but the wind whipped the sound out of his mouth and launched it

37

upwards in the direction of outer space.

The clouds, which had looked like a layer of marshmallow, became wispy and then they plunged through them and Denzel got his first glimpse of New York City. It was only a glimpse because he immediately squeezed his eyes closed, but they were open long enough for him to see hundreds of thousands of buildings spread out below him, with a large rectangle of green positioned near the centre.

"Cor, this is a turn-up for the books, isn't it?" said Smithy, shouting to make himself heard. "I didn't see this coming."

Whoops, sorry, said the voice in Denzel's head. *One minute.*

"Everyone looks like ants," Smithy commented, but Denzel refused to open his eyes to check.

Got you, the voice said, then the wind fell away as the world flipped upside down.

Denzel opened his eyes to find himself much closer to the ground now. He was falling past tall buildings and could see himself reflected in their many windows as he tumbled down, down, down towards the traffic-jammed street below.

No. This time, said the voice, and everything flipped again.

A *thoom* rang out as Denzel landed on something metallic.

Three seconds later, Smithy landed on top of him. They flailed about in a tangle of arms and legs for a moment, before Denzel jumped to his feet. "We're alive!"

"Speak for yourself," said Smithy.

"*I'm alive*! And I'm not even hurt!" Denzel cried.

His head slammed into the room's low ceiling and the whole place echoed with a metallic *thump*.

"Ow!" he yelped, covering his head with his hands. It was at that point that he realised they weren't in a room at all. They were in a van.

"Hey, you made it!"

Denzel and Smithy both whipped round to find a girl grinning at them from the van's front seat, which was turned one hundred and eighty degrees away from the steering wheel and black-tinted windscreen.

Or, at least, she was grinning vaguely in their direction. She had what looked like a virtual reality headset fixed to the top half of her face, and her smile was actually pointed a metre or so to Denzel's left.

"Sorry about the mid-air thing. Forgot to recalibrate. Still, you're here now."

"What? What's going on?" Denzel demanded. "How did we get here? We were in the airport, then we were in the sky, then—"

"You teleported," said the girl. "I teleported you."

"Into mid-air?!"

"Yeah, that was my bad. Sorry."

Denzel shook his head, her words just filtering through the shroud of panic that clouded his brain. "What do you mean, 'teleported'?"

"I mean you teleported. Well ... kinda. Teleported, fell through a gap in the fabric of reality. It depends on your point of view, really. The important thing is, you're here now, and none of your atoms are mixed up."

She adjusted a dial on the side of her headset. "They aren't, are they?"

"No!" said Denzel. He looked himself up and down. "I mean, I don't think so. Who are you?"

"More important than *that*," said Smithy. "Is this a van?" He leaned the top half of his body out through the side, looked around for a moment, then pulled it back in. "It is," he confirmed. "It's a van. It's definitely a van. I knew it."

"What are you doing? Someone could have seen you," said Denzel.

"Nah. We're in a ... what do you call it?"

"Van?" Denzel guessed.

"No, the other one," said Smithy. "Alleyway. There's no

40

one around."

The girl nodded. The extra weight of the VR kit seemed to make it quite tricky, and her head sort of flopped up and down a bit in quite an awkward way. "Yeah, I made sure we were tucked out of sight, just in case anything went wrong with the transport."

"You mean in case our atoms merged," said Denzel.

"Yeah. That. Or, you know. Anything ... explosive," said the girl. She pushed the headset backwards off her head, revealing a short crop of ginger hair, a mass of freckles and the greenest eyes Denzel had ever seen. "I'm Weinberg," she said. "Ada Weinberg."

She held out a hand for Denzel to shake, realised it was covered in oil, and gave it a quick wipe on the blue and silver camo of her Vulteron uniform before extending it again.

"Welcome to New York!"

One short ride and a quite staggering amount of horn-honking later, Denzel and Smithy stepped out of the back of the van on to a narrow road between two rows of tall buildings. As Denzel's feet hit the pavement, a delicious sugary smell simultaneously hit his nostrils, instantly making his mouth water.

"Doughnuts," he said, sniffing the air. The last thing

he'd eaten had been a bag of peanuts on the plane, and those had tasted stale. His stomach gurgled loudly enough to temporarily drown out the sound of traffic thundering past at both ends of the narrow street.

"We'll leave the van here," said Weinberg, hopping down beside them. She pressed a button on her key ring and a series of locks slid into place inside the vehicle. "You can't be too careful," she explained. Then, to Denzel's disappointment, she marched straight past the doughnut shop, heading for the much busier street that ran at right angles to the one they were on.

Yellow cabs, white vans and a *lot* of people criss-crossed past the mouth of the side road, honking and revving and shouting. It was like everyone and every*thing* was angry, and no one really knew why.

"Should you go out there dressed like that?" asked Denzel, gesturing to Weinberg's uniform.

"It's New York City," Weinberg said. "I could go out there in a monkey-suit and a tutu, and no one would bat an eyelid."

She stepped out of the side street and into the throng of pedestrians. Sure enough, none of them gave her so much as a second look. "Now, come on," she said. "It's just round here."

Smithy and Denzel followed her on to the street and

were immediately struck by the scale of it all. Buildings stretched to the sky on all sides, making the street feel like the floor of an enormous canyon.

Even without moving his head, Denzel reckoned he could see more people than he'd seen in his whole life up to that point. There were thousands of them – tens of thousands, maybe – all rushing around like they should have been somewhere important five minutes ago and were going to be in big trouble once they got there.

"Hey, I know this place," said Smithy, as Weinberg stopped outside a building with three sets of doors. The number 350 was fixed above the middle door, while the revolving doors on the left and right were marked "Observatory Exit" and "Observatory Entrance" respectively. "This was in that film."

"What film?" asked Denzel.

"The one with that woman in it," said Smithy. "And the planes are shooting at her at the end."

"The one with the woman in it?" Denzel muttered. "That narrows it down."

Denzel leaned back and looked up at the building.

And up.

And up.

There, emblazoned in gold twenty or more metres above the doors, were two block-printed words.

"Empire State".

"Did it also have a massive gorilla in it?" Denzel asked.

Smithy rubbed his chin thoughtfully. "Hmm. Don't think so."

"Are you sure? It wasn't *King Kong*?"

"That's it!" said Smithy. "I saw it when it first came out. Don't remember a big gorilla though."

"The big gorilla was the whole point!" Denzel said. "They take the gorilla from the island, it gets loose in New York, grabs a woman and climbs up the Empire State Building with her. Then they shoot him."

"Spoilers!" Smithy protested.

"You've already seen it," Denzel reminded him.

"Oh. Yeah," said Smithy. "Man, I loved that film."

Weinberg grinned and pushed open the middle door. "You think the movie was good? You should have been there for the real thing."

Denzel and Smithy both stared after her, then followed her inside. "Wait a minute, wait a minute," said Denzel. "Are you telling me *King Kong* was *real*?"

They had entered a grand hallway, which appeared to be made entirely from marble. A carving of the Empire State Building was fixed to the wall at the far end. An old man in a red jacket sat behind a desk in front of it, nodding and smiling as a tourist in a hat shaped like a big apple fired questions at him.

"Well, not exactly, but most of it, yeah. Not that I was there, of course. Before my time." She headed for one of the two sets of lift doors near the desk. Ropes had been placed for people to queue up, but there was barely anyone around at the moment. Weinberg gave the old man at the desk a wave as she passed. "Harvey."

"Ada," he said, smiling one of the widest, most beaming smiles Denzel had ever seen. "You folks have a good day now."

The lift doors opened. Weinberg led Denzel and Smithy inside, then pressed a complex sequence of buttons on the elevator controls. The doors began to close, but were stopped when the tourist in the big apple hat jammed an arm between them, forcing them to spring open again.

"Hey there!" he said. "Going up?"

"No, sorry," said Weinberg. "We're going down."

"Down?" said the man. "There's a down?" But before he could get an answer, the doors closed with a *ping* and the elevator rumbled down into the bowels of New York City.

CHAPTER 6

Denzel wasn't an expert in geography. In fact, he wouldn't even consider himself an amateur at it. The truth was, he barely really thought about the subject at all.

He knew north was sort of *up the way*, and that countries closer to the equator were hotter than those further away (although he could never remember the word "equator" and instead just called it "the middle bit").

He knew that water went down plugholes the opposite way in the southern hemisphere, but only because he'd seen it on an episode of *The Simpsons*. He knew there was a Great Wall in China, some Pyramids in Egypt, and three chip shops in his home town, all within walking distance.

The three chip shops were within walking distance *of each other*, that is – not within walking distance of the Great Wall of China or the Egyptian Pyramids. At least, Denzel didn't think they were, but then, as has already been established, geography wasn't really his strong point.

What he did know was that New York was one of the biggest cities on the planet, and hundreds of years old. Ghost activity in a place so old and huge would have to be through the roof, Denzel reckoned. Considering how big a branch of the Spectre Collectors was based in his little home town, he couldn't wait to see how epic the New York branch was.

The lift rumbled to a stop.

"You ready for this?" asked Weinberg.

Denzel and Smithy both nodded. "Ready."

The door opened. Denzel stepped out first, then stared in disbelief at the vast army spread out before him.

The ranks were made of oddly misshapen creatures, all wielding axes and spears, and kitted out in rusty old suits of armour. A legion of decaying zombies and bleached skeletons were shambling into attack in a pincer movement, which threatened to tear the army in two.

"Finally!" said a stocky, lank-haired boy through a mouthful of doughnut. "It's your turn, Weinberg. My undead army is going to rip your lot to pieces."

Weinberg stepped out of the elevator, glanced briefly at the battlefield spread out on the tabletop, then took a small stack of cards from her front pocket and flicked through them.

While he waited, Denzel looked around the room they had emerged into. It was a basement. Just an ordinary old basement, with bare light bulbs hanging from the ceiling, stacks of cardboard boxes piled in the corner, and ancient-looking pipework running horizontally across one wall.

On the wall opposite was a haphazardly arranged book case, a map of the city (dated 1972) and a metal filing cabinet that had been bound around each drawer with lengths of willow. Based on what little he knew about ... well, anything, really, Denzel guessed that was where they stored the gems that held all the trapped ghosts.

"I'll play Gartron's Rewind," Weinberg announced, tossing one of the cards on to the table. "So you have to move all your platoons back to the start of your previous turn."

The boy swallowed his doughnut, then wiped his

mouth on the sleeve of his Oberon robe. "But that's going to take me ages!" he protested. "I've got over a hundred figures there." He raised his eyes to Denzel. "All hand-painted."

"Um, well done," said Denzel, which seemed to be the answer the boy was looking for. He reached across the battlefield and shook Denzel's hand.

"Martinez. Joseph Martinez. I'm Weinberg's partner."

"Uh, yeah. Hi. Denzel."

Martinez smiled, then scraped the last of the doughnut mush from his teeth with his tongue. "Yeah. Yeah, I know who you are! We've heard all about you. You're a celebrity. I can't believe you've graced us with your presence."

Smithy held a hand out for Martinez to shake, but the Oberon boy let out a little *cheep* and drew back. "Don't hurt me," he yelped, then he quickly tried to compose himself. "I mean, uh, hello. You're the ... the..."

"Ghost," said Denzel.

"But just call me Smithy."

Swallowing nervously, Martinez reached across the table and gave Smithy's offered hand a brief, half-hearted shake.

"You feel normal," he muttered, then he shook his head. "I mean ... I mean, I wasn't sure what... Forget it."

Martinez looked down and quickly began moving all his zombies and skeletons back across the table. Denzel scanned the room around them again.

"So," he asked. "Where's everyone else?"

Martinez and Weinberg exchanged a glance. "Uh, everyone else?" said Martinez.

"Yeah, you know." Denzel gestured around the cramped basement. "Everyone else. The other Spectre Collectors."

"It's just us," said Weinberg.

This time it was Denzel and Smithy's turn to swap confused looks. "You what?" said Denzel. "I don't understand. This is New York, isn't it?"

"Yep," confirmed Weinberg.

"It is," agreed Smithy.

"And New York's huge."

"One of the biggest cities on Earth," said Weinberg.

"Massive," added Smithy.

"And people must die here, like all the time."

"Constantly."

Smithy sniffed, as if fighting back tears. "It's tragic, really."

"So...?"

"So what?" asked Martinez, briefly looking up from where he was redeploying his army of ghouls.

"So why aren't there more of you?" said Denzel. "I mean, this place must be full of ghosts."

Smithy's eyes darted sideways. Denzel didn't even need to look to know. "Not this specific room, Smithy," he clarified. "I meant the city."

Weinberg shrugged and fished around in a little sink until she'd found the cleanest mug. She ran it under the tap as she talked. "It was. It used to be crazy. You could hardly walk down Lex without something manifesting, and you did *not* want to be caught in Central Park after dark."

"You still don't," added Martinez. "But for very different reasons."

"Bears?" said Smithy. "Is it bears? I bet it's bears."

Martinez laughed a little too hard, like he was scared of offending Smithy. "Haha! *Bears!*" he said, then he went back to repositioning his plastic army.

"So what happened?" asked Denzel. "Where did they go?"

Weinberg wiped her mug on her uniform, then inserted it into some kind of machine. Some kind of coffee machine, Denzel supposed, although it wasn't like any other he'd ever seen. It looked like several drinks machines – and possibly a small vacuum cleaner – were attempting to exist in the same place at the same time, and all of them were losing the fight.

Wires and hoses and angular bits of plastic jutted out in a variety of directions. There were dozens of dials, buttons and switches, as well as a yellow and black lever with a hand-written sign warning "DO NOT TOUCH" taped above it. Another sign below it added: "SERIOUSLY, DON'T!"

Weinberg swivelled her finger above the buttons, as if looking for the right option, then jabbed one and jumped back. Almost immediately, the machine began to rattle, shudder and hiss. Clouds of steam rose from the mouth of one of the pipes, and Martinez had to scramble to catch all his little soldiers as the machine's vibrations made them dance across the tabletop.

"They went the same place as all ghosts round here," Weinberg shouted, struggling to make herself heard over the din of the machine.

"AND WHERE'S THAT?" Denzel bellowed back. The machine stopped right after his first word, and his voice boomed out in the sudden silence.

"All right, all right, no need to scream the place down," Smithy told him.

Weinberg took her mug from the machine, sniffed it, then took a sip. Her face contorted in disgust for a moment, then she shuddered violently. "Want one?"

she asked, pointing to the mug.

"Uh, no," said Denzel. "We're fine. So where did all the ghosts go?"

Weinberg pointed upwards. Denzel and Smithy both looked at the ceiling.

"Well, I hate to tell you, but they're not there now," Smithy said.

"No, not the ceiling," said Martinez. "The spike."

Denzel frowned. "The spike?"

"Yeah," said Weinberg, her mouth curving into a smile. "The spike."

Smithy looked between them all. "Should I say 'the spike' now too? Is that what we're doing?"

"What's the spike?" Denzel asked.

"All in good time," said Weinberg. "But first..." She rummaged in a drawer until she found a folded leaflet. It had a photo of a pizza on the front. "Who's hungry?"

Denzel stood in the foyer of the Empire State Building, shuffling from foot to foot and clicking his fingers as he waited for the pizzas to arrive. Martinez and Weinberg were tidying a space for them all to sit and eat, and had asked Smithy to stay and help them. Denzel hadn't been particularly in favour of the idea – Martinez didn't exactly seem relaxed in Smithy's company – but Smithy had assured him he'd be fine.

Harvey, the guy behind the desk, flashed Denzel a warm smile and Denzel smiled back. He thought about going over and asking him some questions about the building they were in, but then decided he probably got enough of those all day, every day, and might appreciate the peace.

"He is coming," Harvey called across to him.

Denzel raised his eyebrows. "Huh? Sorry, what?"

Just then, one of the revolving doors spun and a gangly teenage boy with long hair and braces on his teeth hurried in, a motorcycle helmet under one arm. Balanced on the other hand were two of the largest pizza boxes Denzel had ever seen. They were two of the largest *anything* boxes he'd ever seen, for that matter.

"Weinberg?" the boy asked.

"No, Denzel."

The boy tutted, looked around the foyer, then turned away.

"Wait, no, actually I *am* Weinberg," said Denzel. "I got confused. I mean, she sent me. I mean..." He thrust out a wad of dollar bills Weinberg had given him. "Here."

The delivery boy regarded him with suspicion for a moment, then shrugged and – with some clever manoeuvring – swapped the money for the pizzas.

Denzel had to use both hands to hold them, and lean back to counter the weight.

The boy rifled through the notes, then met Denzel's eye. "Uh, what about a tip?"

Denzel hesitated. "Uh, like a sightseeing tip? That'd be great, thanks. The magazine I read on the plane said to try to get some local knowledge on where to go and what to see."

"No! What you talkin' about? I mean like a tip that *you* give *me*."

"Oh," said Denzel. "Oh. Right." He thought for a moment. "Uh, don't eat yellow snow?"

He nodded at the stunned-looking delivery boy, then headed for the lift, struggling to see over the enormous pizza boxes. As he neared the doors, Harvey jumped up from his seat and tapped the button to open them.

"Thanks," said Denzel. He tried to walk through, but the boxes got jammed on either side of the opening. He had to tilt them sideways to fit through.

It was only when he was inside that he remembered the instructions Weinberg had given him on how to send the lift down were still in his back pocket. He tried to think of a way to make them leap out of his pocket and into his hand, but came up blank.

"Allow me," said Harvey, leaning in. The old man's

withered fingers tapped lightly across the buttons, then he leaned out through the doors and smiled.

"Thanks," said Denzel.

The old man's smile fell away. His eyes became glassy and lifeless, like a doll's, as the doors began to close.

"He is coming," said Harvey in a low, scratchy whisper. "He. Is. Comi—"

The lift doors closed, and Harvey was replaced by Denzel's open-mouthed reflection. "OK," he whispered as the lift began to descend. "What was that about?"

The lift jerked when it reached the bottom, almost making Denzel drop the pizza boxes. He frantically scrambled to hold on to them, and only managed to stop them falling by jamming them between his chest and one of the lift's walls.

The doors slid aside and – after a few attempts – he made it out. "I got the pizzas," he announced, in case the two huge boxes with "Pizza" written on the side weren't enough of a clue.

To Denzel's surprise, the basement was empty. No Weinberg. No Martinez. No Smithy.

"Uh, hello?"

He noticed a door he hadn't spotted before. It was tucked into the darkest corner of the basement, half hidden by the gloom. The only reason Denzel had seen it this time was because it stood ajar, showing a strip of the brightly lit room beyond.

From within the room, Denzel heard Smithy's voice, sharp and sudden and shocked.

"No," Smithy yelped. "No!"

Denzel hurled the pizzas boxes on to the table, completely failing to notice when they scattered the little plastic armies and slid on to the floor. He should never have left his friend down here alone. A ghost, all by himself with two ghost-hunters. What was he thinking?

"I'm coming, Smithy! I'm coming!" Denzel bellowed, then he clenched his fists, lowered his head and threw himself at the door.

CHAPTER 7

Denzel hurtled through the door with his fists windmilling.

"I'm here, Smithy!" he cried, although midway through the statement he realised his dramatic entrance probably wasn't necessary. Smithy didn't seem to be in any immediate danger. Or any danger at all, in fact.

This room was smaller than the other one, but much tidier and more brightly lit. Martinez was "setting" a rectangular metal table that took up a full half of the room. This seemed to involve just dumping three uneven piles of paper napkins down on it, but even that seemed to take a lot of effort on his part.

Smithy and Weinberg stood in front of a tall glass cylinder that had been bound dozens of times with willow-tree branches. A red gem was suspended in the middle of the cylinder, apparently by magic.

Denzel had learned a little bit about the gems from his training. They were used to hold captured ghosts inside, stopping them getting out and wreaking havoc. This one was by far the largest gem Denzel had seen though. The ones back home had been a third of the size, maybe less.

"Hey, Denzel!" said Smithy. He pointed to the gem in the tube. "Check this out!"

Denzel approached the glass. "What is it?"

"That, my friend, is King Kong!" said Smithy.

Denzel shook his head in disbelief. "No. No."

"That's just what I said!" Smithy laughed. "But it is!" He nudged Weinberg. "Tell him."

"It isn't King Kong," Weinberg said.

"See!" said Smithy. "Wait, what?"

"That was just the name they gave him in the movie. His real name is Kongraueri."

"We should probably just call him 'King Kong'," Smithy suggested. "Easier, innit?"

Denzel leaned in closer to the glass, but cautiously, as if the gem inside it might explode at any moment. "And the rest of the story? How much was true?"

"Quite a bit, actually," said Weinberg. "I mean, not the Skull Island or fighting dinosaur stuff, but the bits in New York weren't far from the truth."

Denzel was so close his breath fogged the glass. The gem sparkled in the overhead lights, but there seemed to be another light, too, pulsing deep within the stone's heart. "The Empire State Building? The woman?"

"Yeah, both those," Weinberg confirmed. "Turns out Kongraueri—"

"King Kong," Smithy corrected.

"Turns out he's fascinated by blonde hair. Maybe it makes him think of bananas or something. The woman was one of our agents. She volunteered to be the bait."

"Nice of her," said Smithy.

"And a bit mad," said Denzel.

"Obviously," Smithy agreed.

Weinberg shrugged. "We do what we have to do to get the job done. Oh, and Kong wasn't shot down by helicopters. The spike took care of him."

Denzel placed a hand against the glass. The pulsing light inside the gemstone seemed to sense him. It squirmed and wriggled, as if trying to get free. Denzel lowered his hand and stepped back. "What is this spike, exactly?"

"I told you, all in good time," Weinberg said. She

clapped her hands together, then looked him up and down. "So. Pizza?"

Denzel looked down at his empty arms, as if only just now realising he wasn't still carrying the boxes. "Oh!" he said, then he spun on his heels and dashed back into the main room. He searched the table for the boxes, then finally found them lying upside down on the floor behind it.

Carefully, he managed to lift the boxes without the lids flopping open. That was the good news. The bad news was that several platoons of zombies, skeletons and other lovingly hand-painted soldiers had been crushed beneath the pizzas' weight. It looked like the aftermath of a great battle, but one that hadn't actually been all that great for the people fighting in it. Mind you, he wondered if battles ever were.

"Oh, no," Denzel whispered.

"Hurry up, we're starving!" Martinez called.

"Coming!" said Denzel. He straightened up and stepped back. A skeletal horse went *crunch* beneath his foot. He quickly stepped away in fright, and a pair of troll-like creatures with spears met their untimely ends beneath his heel.

He turned with another two crunches. The pizza boxes made it impossible to see the floor, so he took a couple of big strides, hoping to cut down the chances of crushing anything else.

No such luck. Something small went *crick*. Something large went *crack*. But then, to his relief, Denzel made it clear of the debris field. With a tilt of the pizzas, he scurried through the door, not daring to glance back at the floor behind him.

"What kept you?" asked Martinez.

"Yes! Hahaha!" said Denzel. He stopped abruptly when he realised this was a completely nonsensical response, darted his eyes around the room, then held up the slightly bashed boxes. "Pizzas."

"Now you're talking," said Weinberg. The table would barely have been big enough for one of the boxes, so she gestured to the floor beside it. With some difficulty, Denzel managed to set the boxes down on the floor.

Weinberg squatted down and hungrily lifted the lid of one of the boxes. She blinked in surprise when she saw the pizza had almost no topping, before spotting it all clinging to the top layer of cardboard in a congealed mass of cheese and pepperoni.

"What happened?" she asked.

Denzel leaned over and looked down. "Huh," he said. "Look at that. I have no idea what could have happened."

"Did you drop it?" asked Martinez.

Denzel just stared at the Oberon boy for a while. "Yep," he admitted. "That might be it."

"Maybe the other one's better," said Weinberg, flipping open the other box. She closed it immediately. "No, that's worse. Not to worry."

She lifted the box containing the less damaged pizza and placed it on the table. Then she fished four big dessert-sized spoons from a little drawer on the table's underside, and handed them out. "Dig in, I guess!"

They spent the next ten minutes scooping blobs of cheesy mush from the lid of the box and depositing it on to the untopped pizza slices. Even though it wasn't exactly in perfect condition, it was still one of the best pizzas Denzel had ever tasted. Smithy, however, didn't look impressed.

"It's a bit... What's the word I'm looking for?"

"Squashed?" Weinberg guessed.

"No, it's a bit..."

"Big?" said Denzel.

"Italian," said Smithy. "It's a bit Italian."

"Well, it should be. Obese Tony *is* Italian," said Martinez, smoothing a small mound of mozzarella and sliced meat over his pizza with the back of his spoon.

"Who's Obese Tony?" Denzel asked.

"The guy who owns the shop," said Weinberg. "He

used to be Fat Tony, but, well … guess he sampled the merchandise one too many times."

"Why would an Italian open a pizza shop?" asked Smithy.

"Er, because pizzas come from Italy?" said Denzel.

Smithy choked on his mouthful of pizza, then coughed so violently it plastered across the remaining slices with a *splat*.

"Aw, Smithy, seriously?" said Denzel. "I was going to eat that."

"Since when were pizzas Italian?" said Smithy.

"Since always," said Martinez. He flinched slightly when Smithy looked at him. "I mean … I think."

Smithy's expression was one of utter disbelief. "Well, what's the one from India then?"

"Curry?" said Weinberg.

Smithy clicked his fingers. "Right. That's it. And this is…?"

"Pizza," said Denzel.

"Gotcha," said Smithy. "I did wonder why it tasted different. I have very sensitive taste buds."

"No, you don't," said Denzel. "I've literally watched you eat cold scrambled egg out of a paper bag."

"Sensitively," said Smithy. He gestured down to the rest of the pizza. The mouthful he'd spat out lay in clumps across it. "Mind if I take another slice?"

"Help yourself," said Weinberg.

"Yeah, knock yourself out," said Martinez. They both watched Smithy cram another slice into his mouth. "Uh, by the way – if you don't mind me asking – how do you eat?"

"Mmmng," said Smithy, chewing quickly. He pointed to his mouth. "Nn mns."

Everyone watched him chew. It went on for quite some time. He pointed to his mouth again and raised his eyebrows, then nodded his head as he tried to chew faster.

Then, with a final few chomps, he swallowed. "What?" he said.

Martinez swallowed too, but nervously. "I was just wondering, how do you eat?"

"With my mouth, mostly," said Smithy. "Sort of, hands first, pop it in the mouth—"

"No, I mean, you're a ghost. How do you eat? *Why* do you eat?"

"Because it tastes good," said Smithy. "I love a good curry."

"Pizza," Denzel corrected.

"Oh, yeah. Yeah, they're not bad either."

Martinez crossed his arms and leaned back. "It's just...

It's weird," he said. "We were taught that ghosts were the bad guys, and now... And now you! There's a ghost in the Spectre Collectors. An actual ghost!"

"Smithy helped stop the Spectral Realm breaking open," said Denzel. "Without him, we'd all be dead now. Or undead. Or ... I don't know. Something, anyway."

Denzel would have been the first to admit his response had fallen apart a bit towards the end, but he reckoned he managed to get his point across, all the same.

Martinez shook his head. "No, I mean, it's ... interesting, that's all. A ghost. An *actual* ghost."

"You're acting like you haven't seen one before," said Denzel.

"Funny you should say that," said Weinberg. She smiled across the table at Denzel and Smithy. "I think it's time we showed you guys the spike."

CHAPTER 8

Denzel pressed himself flat against the smooth stone wall. His eyes were screwed tightly closed, as a wind whistled and wailed around him.

Less than a metre in front of him was a small wall, barely fifty centimetres high, and beyond that...

Well, he didn't really want to think what was beyond that right now. If he did, there was a very good chance he'd wet himself, pass out or do both of those things simultaneously.

"This is the one hundred and third floor," Weinberg explained. "It's the highest point on the whole building. Y'know, if you don't count the spike."

"Wow, the ground is a long way away, isn't it?" said Smithy. "Look, Denzel. Denzel, look. Look, Denzel. Look at it, Denzel."

"Shut up!" Denzel yelped, then he pressed himself harder against the wall. "How is this allowed? This can't be safe."

"Depends," said Weinberg.

Denzel opened one eye. "On what?"

"On if you fall off or not," Weinberg said. She grinned. "It's fine, you're perfectly safe. I won't let anything happen to you. Take a look."

Denzel tried to summon the courage to detach himself from the wall, but his body overruled him. It did allow him to open his other eye though, as long as he kept facing straight ahead and didn't even *think* about looking down.

It was a compromise he could live with. He'd already got a pretty good bird's-eye view of the city when he'd been plunging towards it from above the clouds, and he didn't really want to see it again. Besides, he didn't really need to look down to see it. The city spread out before him for miles in every direction. Night was closing in and the buildings were ablaze with lights of every conceivable colour.

This high up there was no sound from the streets

below, and Denzel almost felt like he was floating in outer space, gazing out over some vast, newly discovered galaxy.

"Imagine falling off," said Smithy, breaking the spell. "Like, imagine you tripped and just went flying over the edge. I wonder how long it'd take to hit the bottom?"

Weinberg shrugged. "Well, taking into account wind resistance, it'd take roughly eight seconds to hit a terminal velocity of a hundred and twenty-two miles per hour, which is … what? Fifty-four metres per second?"

"About that, yeah," said Smithy, who had absolutely no idea.

"We're around four hundred and forty-three metres in the air at the moment…"

Denzel let out a high-pitched *cheep* of fear.

"So I guess around … eleven seconds?" said Weinberg.

"And then … splat!" said Smithy.

"Yeah. Kind of," said Weinberg. "Although, when you factor in mass and bone density of the average human being and the like, it'd be more of a *crunch*. Now, a horse – a horse would go *splat*."

Smithy nodded slowly. "How would we get a horse up the stairs though?"

"I wasn't actually suggesting we throw a horse off the top of the Empire State Building," said Weinberg. "I'm just saying, if we did—"

"Please stop talking!" Denzel whimpered.

"What's wrong?" asked Smithy. "Why are you shaking? Are you cold? You're cold, aren't you? I think he's cold."

Denzel shook his head. He *was* actually pretty cold – the wind was bitter up there – but it wasn't so much the chill that was making him shake; more the overwhelming sense of eye-popping terror he was currently experiencing.

He'd never really been all that bothered by heights before, but then he didn't think he'd ever been this high up.

OK, technically the plane had been much higher than this, and the whole teleporting into mid-air thing, and he'd recently flown above his home town in a suit made entirely of ghosts, but this was different somehow. On all three of those occasions, what happened next had been pretty much out of his control. Now, though, his life depended on him not doing anything stupid. One slip, one small error of judgement, and – eleven-ish seconds later – his body would quite closely resemble his last meal.

Smithy slapped him hard across the face. Denzel gaped at him, his mouth hanging open. "Ow! What did you do that for?"

"You looked like you were panicking," said Smithy.

"I *was* panicking!" Denzel confirmed. "And I'm still panicking, only now my face hurts."

"Oh," said Smithy. "Right."

He thought for a moment, then slapped Denzel again.

"Cut it out! Stop hitting me!" Denzel yelped.

"Should I kick you in the leg?"

"No!"

"I could knee you in the—"

"Don't do anything!" Denzel said. "It's not helping."

Smithy shrugged. "Suit yourself. Don't say I didn't offer."

Denzel's eyes darted to Weinberg. "Why did you bring us up here?"

Weinberg pointed up. "The spike," she said. Denzel's body reluctantly let him move his head, but took a moment to stress the importance of not looking down, just in case he'd forgotten. He hadn't.

A small stone ledge hung above Denzel's head, blocking his view.

"You can't see it from there," Weinberg said. "You have to step out a bit."

"Not going to happen," said Denzel. "Describe it."

"It's like... Have you ever seen pictures of this building?"

Denzel nodded.

"You know that spiky bit on the top?"

Denzel nodded.

"It's that."

Denzel's nostrils flared. His lips went thin. "You dragged us all the way up here for *that*?"

"I thought you'd want to see it," said Weinberg.

"Nope!" Denzel said, his voice coming out as a squeak. "Definitely don't."

"OK, well, short version then. When Kong was on his rampage it became clear there was no way of capturing him with the weapons available at the time," Weinberg explained. "So one of my predecessors – *our* predecessors, I guess – found a way of building a Spectral Resonance Unit right into the building's antenna."

"Clever, that's just what I'd have done," said Smithy, then: "What's a Spectral Resonance Unit?"

"Uh... Think of it as a vacuum cleaner, but for ghosts," said Weinberg. "Anything made up of Spectral Energy gets too close and – zip – the spike pulls it in."

"Anything?" said Smithy. He gripped on to the low railing fixed to the top of the wall.

"Relax," said Weinberg. "It hasn't worked in years. Better Vulterons than me have tried to fix it, but it's kaput. It worked on Kong though, which was the point. And then, over the next forty years or so, before it broke down, it just sort of drained all the Spectral Energy from the city. Nowadays New York is pretty much a ghost-free zone. That's why Martinez may have been acting a little … weird earlier." She shot Smithy an apologetic look. "See, we don't have much experience with actual ghosts, as such. In fact, I don't even remember the last time we got a—"

A walkie-talkie on the girl's belt crackled into life. "Uh, Weinberg," said Martinez. "We just got a call. Over."

Weinberg frowned, but it was a good-natured one, like she'd just been told a joke she didn't yet understand. "From who? Over."

"No. I mean we got *a call*," said Martinez. "Over."

"Oh," said Weinberg. She looked Denzel and Smithy up and down, the radio held motionless in front of her mouth. "Well, this can't be a coincidence. We'll be right down. Over."

She clipped the walkie-talkie back on to her belt. "OK, so that's weird," she said. "It seems there *are* some ghosts left in New York City, after all. I guess we'd better go to work."

73

CHAPTER 9

"It happened through there. But I'm telling you, I ain't ever seen nothin' like it."

The man standing before the locked double doors was old and burly, with dirty calloused hands that had spent a lifetime punching people in the head and upper body. His nose was a misshapen bump in the middle of his face and his ears looked like they'd been made out of Play-Doh.

The call had come via a contact in the mayor's office. A boxing gym in an area of New York called Brooklyn was reporting some highly unusual activity, and while Weinberg assumed it'd be a false alarm, they'd all come along to check anyway.

"And what's through there, sir?" asked Weinberg.

"The pool."

"As in...?" Smithy mimed hitting a pool ball with a cue.

"As in *swimming* pool," said the man.

"Gotcha. Thanks for clearing that up, Jim," said Smithy.

"My name ain't Jim. It's Arnold."

"Oh," said Smithy, slightly taken aback. "Then who's Jim?"

"He runs a gym," said Denzel, gesturing at the empty hall behind them, filled with punch bags, weight benches and a full-size boxing ring.

"That's probably why he's getting confused," said Smithy.

Arnold, who hadn't previously been confused at all – but was rapidly starting to be – frowned. "What are you talking about?" he asked. "Who are you anyway? You don't look like city officials. You ain't old enough."

"We're older than we look," said Martinez.

Smithy pointed to Denzel. "He's fifty-seven."

Arnold shook his head. "OK, get out," he said, moving to push them aside. Martinez placed a hand in the middle of the man's broad chest. A yellow light briefly crackled from the Oberon's fingertips.

"I think we should take a look around," said Martinez.

Arnold stopped. He blinked slowly. "Yeah. Yeah, you should take a look around."

"Thank you," said Martinez. He removed his hand, then turned back to the others and winked as Arnold unlocked the doors behind him.

A wave of heat rolled out – that type of heat you only ever get around indoor swimming pools that immediately makes your back start sweating. Arnold shambled through. Weinberg and Martinez went next, with Denzel and Smithy tagging along at the back.

The pool was around the size of a tennis court, perhaps a little smaller. Light rippled and danced across the windowless walls, picking out details Denzel reckoned would have been better off hidden.

The room the pool was housed in was old and dirty, with black mildew on the tiles and rings of damp up on the ceiling. The floor tiles were chipped, cracked or – in some cases – missing completely. A weed grew in the gap between two of the grubbier tiles. By the looks of it, it had been there a while.

It was the first swimming pool Denzel had ever seen where drowning was *way* down the list of potential health and safety issues.

"Tell us in your own words what happened," said Weinberg.

Arnold blinked again, as if waking from a dream. "Uh, so there was this noise."

"Definitely ghosts," said Smithy. Martinez shot him an anxious look, then glanced around for danger.

"What kind of noise?" asked Weinberg.

"Like ... a kind of groaning," said Arnold. "You know, like the noise old pipes make when they expand."

Denzel glanced up at the mouldy ceiling. There was a grid of rusty metal pipes criss-crossing over around a third of it.

"And then a kind of ... whispering."

"Ghosts," said Smithy.

"Whispering?" said Weinberg.

"Yeah, you know. Like ... like water swishing through pipes."

"Right. Right," said Weinberg. "It all seems pretty pipe-based at the moment. Maybe a plumber would be a better—"

"And then everyone started floating."

Weinberg hesitated. "In the water?"

Arnold shook his head. "In the air."

"Oh."

"Ghosts," Martinez whispered.

Smithy shrugged. "Well, let's not rush to any conclusions."

Martinez sniffed the air, following his nose until it led him to a gloss-painted wall. Black stains bloomed beneath the paint's shiny glaze. After another few experimental sniffs, he touched his tongue against the paintwork.

Denzel and Smithy both recoiled in disgust. "Ugh what are you doing?" asked Denzel. "That wall looks poisonous." He smiled at Arnold. "No offence."

"I'm definitely getting something," said Martinez.

"Ebola?" Denzel guessed.

"Spectral Energy. Recent."

Weinberg unclipped a small device from her belt. It was a little larger than a mobile phone, with a screen on the front and four short prongs fixed to the top. It let out a short *bleep* when she switched it on...

...and then immediately exploded in her hand with a *bang* that echoed around the windowless room.

"Uh, yeah," she said, flexing her fingers inside her scorched glove. "There is *definitely* Spectral Energy in here." She looked across to the other side of the pool. There were three doors there, all closed. "What's through there?"

Arnold lifted his head slowly and frowned, like he'd never seen the doors before. "Uh, changing rooms and storage," he said, after some thought. He pointed. "Men. Women. Closet."

"We should check them out," said Martinez. "Weinberg, we'll take the changing rooms, one each. You two," he continued, gesturing to Smithy and Denzel. "Maybe you could check the closet?"

"Is that wise?" asked Weinberg. "They're not armed. They might get hurt."

"He's already a ghost," said Martinez, nodding at Smithy.

"Yeah, but Denzel isn't," Weinberg pointed out. "The Elders won't be happy if we get him killed."

"I won't exactly be delighted either," Denzel pointed out.

Weinberg smiled at him. "Relax. You're fine. Smithy, you check out the closet. Denzel, wait here and, uh, make sure no one else comes in."

Denzel and Smithy looked at each other, then shrugged. "OK," said Denzel. He gestured to the door. "I'll try to fight back the hordes."

Martinez gestured for Arnold to lead the way. The old man unhooked a bunch of keys from his belt as he shuffled around the pool. He didn't appear to be even remotely surprised by any of the conversation he'd just heard, but then Martinez seemed to have zapped him with some magic mojo, so that probably helped.

With three echoing *clunks*, the doors were unlocked.

Weinberg and Martinez exchanged a nod, then *creaked* the changing-room doors open and stepped inside. Arnold followed Martinez inside, trotting along behind him like a loyal puppy.

Smithy hesitated at the closet door, turned and gave Denzel a wave, then stepped backwards, slipping cleanly through the peeling paint and damp wood like a – well, like a Smithy.

Denzel shoved his hands down in his pockets and walked slowly along the side of the pool, swinging his feet in wide arcs. He whistled, but the echo was annoying, so he didn't keep it up for long.

He clicked his fingers a few times, then yawned. He couldn't remember when he'd last slept. Today? Yesterday? The day before? Surely not that long ago, but he couldn't really be certain. He tried to figure out what time it would be back home, but he'd forgotten if you added hours on or took them away. He'd have to ask Weinberg and Martinez when they got back.

SSSSSSHHHHK.

Denzel stopped. He looked down at the water, then up at the pipes on the ceiling above him. He listened. He was sure he'd heard … something. A hissing, maybe.

After several seconds he shrugged and went back to pacing again. He was halfway along the poolside when he heard another sound. Definitely a sound, but not a hissing.

A whispering.

He is coming.

The words bounced back at Denzel from all four walls, overlapping until the room was filled with the whispers.

He is coming.

He is coming.

HE IS COMING.

Denzel took his hands out of his pockets, but otherwise froze. He held his breath, managing to keep it in until the whispers faded back into silence. He let the breath out slowly, scared to make a sound. It turned into a cloud of white vapour in front of his mouth, and Denzel felt his skin prickle as a wave of cold air washed over him.

The three doors were still closed. Denzel thought about calling for the others, but that would *definitely* involve making a sound, and he wasn't sure that was such a good idea right now.

Something moved beneath the surface of the pool, sending bubbles rolling to the surface. Denzel's first instinct was to run away and never look back – with some possible screaming in there for good measure – but he planted his feet on the cracked tiles and gritted his teeth.

He shouldn't be scared of ghosts. He was a Spectre Collector, after all. Not being scared of ghosts was pretty much his job now.

Besides, the majority of the ghosts he'd personally encountered had turned out to be pretty decent people. Well, maybe not "people" exactly, but whatever they were, they were mostly nice, all the same.

Sure, during his training he'd heard tales of monstrous horrors that had kept him awake for the better part of a week, hugging his pillow and silently crying, but his personal record with supernatural entities had mostly been a positive one.

Denzel had just about managed to convince himself he had absolutely nothing to worry about when two tendrils of dirty pool water tangled around his throat like vines and yanked him off his feet.

For a tiny moment, Denzel felt as if he were flying, and then he hit the water with a *splash*. The stinging chlorine forced his eyes closed, even as the grip on his throat tightened. He kicked frantically for the surface, his arms thrashing like a paddling dog. The water itself seemed to be dragging him down though, pulling him further and further away from the precious fresh air above.

He'd barely had a moment to gulp down a breath, and already he could feel his lungs cramping up. The tendrils tightened and a worrying number of bubbles escaped through Denzel's nose.

He was becoming disorientated, and could no longer figure out which way he should be swimming. He forced his eyes open and twisted his head, searching for the surface. It was just above him – barely further than his arm could stretch – but there was no way of reaching it.

Through the blur of chlorine, Denzel spotted a shape in the pool with him. It was a large shape. Worryingly large.

Terrifyingly large, in fact.

And it was getting closer.

But, right now, that was the least of Denzel's problems. Pain flared in his lungs. The grip tightened around his throat. His mouth opened with a bubbling gasp, and as the pool water seeped down his throat, Denzel sank slowly into darkness.

CHAPTER 10

"Denzel?"

The voice drifted down from somewhere above. Denzel tried to open his eyes but he was too tired. Was he asleep? Had his alarm gone off? What time was it?

Oh, no. He was dead, wasn't he? That was it. He'd drowned.

"Denzel!"

So why was someone shouting at him? And who kept pressing down on his chest? He wished they'd stop. That last one had almost forced his lungs out through his nose.

Denzel coughed, sneezed, gasped and spluttered at

the same time, ejecting a not insignificant amount of water out through his mouth and nose. He tried to sit up but *clonked* heads with Arnold. The gym owner was leaning over him, the heels of his hands pressed against the middle of Denzel's chest.

Weinberg and Martinez stood above him, both looking worried. As soon as it was clear that Denzel wasn't dead, Smithy barged Arnold aside, sending the old man sprawling on to the tiles.

"Denzel! You're alive!" Smithy cried.

"Am I?" said Denzel, unable to hide his surprise.

"Yes! I mean ... I think so," said Smithy. He looked up at Weinberg. She nodded.

"Good to have you back with us," she said.

"What happened?" asked Martinez.

Denzel's head dropped back, hitting the tiles with a *clunk*. He tried to remember. What *had* happened?

"There was whispering," he said. "And then the water."

Everyone looked at the water, then back to Denzel. "What about the water?" asked Weinberg.

What about it? He couldn't be sure. He'd been in the water, he remembered that much.

But why? Not by choice, surely?

He sat up suddenly.

"There's something in the water!" His voice boomed

around the room, making everyone jump. Denzel scrambled to his feet as everything came flooding back. He remembered the tendrils around his throat, the chlorine in his eyes and the water in his lungs.

And he remembered the shape – enormous and ominous, scything through the water towards him.

"You're right, there is! Look!" yelped Smithy. He pointed to the surface of the pool, where a solitary sticking plaster bobbed around on the gently lapping waves.

Denzel shook his head. "No, it was something ... horrible."

"That's pretty horrible, to be fair," said Smithy.

"No, but it was huge," Denzel insisted. "I think it might have been a sea monster."

Weinberg sidled closer to the edge and leaned over. "Well, it's not there now."

Denzel shook his head. "But it *was* there. I saw it! You've got to believe me."

"Hey, we do believe you," said Weinberg. "Come on, think about who you're talking to here. We'll pretty much believe anything."

Martinez gave the wall another lick. Denzel recoiled again. "Seriously, every time you do that it probably takes ten years off your life."

"Nothing," said Martinez, flicking his tongue in and out of his mouth. "The Spectral Energy is gone."

"Gone?" said Weinberg. "How can it be gone? It should linger for days. Months, even!"

"I know," said Martinez. "But it's gone."

"Hey, what's going on?" demanded Arnold. He was getting back to his feet and looking far less dazed than he had a moment ago. "What are you kids doing in here?"

He looked at Denzel, and at the water dripping from the bottom of his trouser legs. "Were you swimming? Did you go swimming in my pool?"

"Relax," said Martinez. He reached into a pouch that was hooked on to the gold-coloured rope he wore as a belt. When his hand came back out, there was a sprinkling of glittering dust in his palm. Memory dust, Denzel knew. One good sniff and Arnold would forget this whole encounter.

Martinez blew on the dust. Arnold blinked rapidly as it swirled around his head, then up through his nostrils.

His face became slack, his eyes became glazed and the Spectre Collectors agreed that it was probably time to leave.

They were back in the Empire State Building, going

down in the lift when Denzel remembered the little plastic soldiers. In the rush to answer the call, Martinez hadn't spotted them scattered and broken behind the table, but once they got back he was bound to see them.

Maybe he'd think there'd been a break-in, Denzel thought. Although quite why someone would break into the underground lair of a secret ghost-hunting society solely to destroy some toy soldiers, Denzel wasn't sure.

"You all right?" said Smithy.

Denzel blinked. "What? Um, yeah."

"It's just you look a bit strange," said Smithy.

Denzel looked down at himself. He'd got changed in the back of the van while the others waited outside, and all that had been available was a jumble of spare Vulteron and Oberon uniform pieces. He now wore a green robe over blue and silver camo-pattern trousers, which were held up by shiny gold rope. The robe was too big, the trousers were too small and he hadn't even been able to get his feet into the boots.

"Yeah. I noticed," Denzel said.

"No, I meant your face," said Smithy. "You look a bit ... guilty."

"No, I don't," said Denzel.

"You do. Doesn't he?"

Weinberg and Martinez both turned and checked out Denzel's face. He tried to make it look as normal as possible, but only succeeded in contorting it into a sort of weird grimace that wouldn't have looked out of place on a gargoyle.

"He does a bit," Weinberg said.

"Looks more like he's constipated to me," said Martinez. "You constipated, Denzel?"

"No!"

"Long flights can do that to you," Martinez continued.

"I'm not constipated!" Denzel insisted. He gestured to Smithy. "He's right, it's guilt!"

Denzel's eyes widened briefly, then he quickly bit his lip.

"I knew it!" said Smithy. He nudged Denzel with his elbow. "What you feeling guilty about?"

Denzel laughed nervously. "Um..." The lift jolted to a stop. "It's funny you should ask..."

The doors opened with a *ping*. Martinez was the first to step out into the basement. He took three paces, then stopped suddenly, as if his feet had been glued to the floor.

Denzel leaned out and looked past him, to where all the tiny figures lay broken on the floor.

"I, uh, may have accidentally dropped the pizza boxes

on all your little guys."

Martinez didn't respond. He just stood there, completely stock still, his eyes fixed on the carnage.

"Oh, boy," Weinberg said. She held her arm out, stopping Denzel and Smithy getting any closer to her partner. "Hey, Joe. You OK?"

"My army," Martinez whispered. "He broke my army."

"It was an accident," Denzel told him.

"You broke *my army*! Do you have any idea how long it took me to build and paint them all?"

"Forty minutes?" Smithy guessed. Denzel shot him a look and hurriedly shook his head. "Ten years?" said Smithy, having another go. "I don't know. Is it a trick question?"

Denzel stepped past Weinberg's arm and approached Martinez. "Look, uh, Joe, I'm really sorry," he began, but then something crunched under his foot and Martinez let out a high-pitched groan.

His arms flew out in a sudden flurry of activity. The air around him scorched with lines of glowing colour. He mumbled something under his breath and a plume of smoke rose from his feet.

For a moment Denzel thought Martinez had caught fire. He was about to jump on the Oberon's back and wrestle him to the floor when, with a faint *whoosh* that made Denzel's ears pop, Martinez vanished into thin air.

"Oh, great," said Smithy. "You killed him. You upset him so much he exploded."

"What? No! I didn't kill him," said Denzel. "Did I?"

Weinberg shook her head. She and Smithy stepped out of the lift doorway, letting the doors close over behind them. "No, he's not dead. He's just gone to his room."

Denzel looked around the basement. "His room?"

"Floor below," Weinberg explained. "We both have rooms there. We tried to find a couple that you guys could use but, well, time hasn't exactly been kind to the place, and we didn't get much notice you were coming."

She squatted beside the broken figures and picked up a mangled skeleton.

"It was an accident," Denzel said.

"Yeah. I know," said Weinberg. "And he knows it too. It's just that his mom gave him these, and she's ... she's not around any more."

"Oh God," Denzel groaned, letting his head fall into his hands. "Seriously?"

"He'll get over it," said Weinberg. "You know, eventually. When he's, like, a hundred."

She started to pick up the figures, then stopped. "You know what, it's late," she said. "We can get this in the morning. You guys should probably get some rest."

Denzel nodded. "Yeah. I'm pretty tired. Smithy?"

"Yes!" said Smithy, grinning broadly. "I'm *dead beat.*"

"Right," said Denzel.

"You know, because I'm dead."

"Gotcha."

"As in, a ghost."

"Yes. I get it," said Denzel. He turned to Weinberg. "So, uh, if we don't have rooms, where are we going to sleep?"

Weinberg spent a few seconds searching through some piles of junk on an old metal shelving unit, then tossed Denzel and Smithy a rolled-up sleeping bag each. She gestured to the room where they'd eaten the pizza. "Knock yourself out."

Then, with a smile and a little salute, she called the lift, stepped inside and the doors slid closed between them.

Smithy unrolled his sleeping bag with a single flick. The material was caked with dried mud, and frayed around the edges. Something rolled out and hit the floor. It was a dead cockroach.

"This is going to be fun, isn't it?" said Smithy.

"Yeah." Denzel sighed, tucking his sleeping bag under his arm. "Terrific."

Two hours later Denzel lay curled up in his sleeping bag

on the hard vinyl floor, trying to get comfortable on a pillow he'd made from a rolled-up Oberon robe.

"Denzel."

Denzel groaned. "What?"

"You awake?"

"No."

"Oh."

There was silence for a few seconds. Denzel heard Smithy shuffle around in his sleeping bag.

"It's just, you sound awake."

"What is it, Smithy?" Denzel asked. "It's four o'clock in the morning."

It wasn't four o'clock in the morning, actually. Or, it might have been. Denzel had no idea. It certainly *felt* like four o'clock in the morning though, and that was the main thing.

"What would you rather, right?"

Denzel let out a sob.

"Have a little screen in one eye so you were always watching a complete stranger go about their life. You know, just watching them do stuff all day. Eat their dinner, go for a poo – everything."

Denzel let out another sob. He hoped Smithy might take the hint. No such luck.

"*Or* not have that, but know someone was always

watching *you* in a little screen in their eye instead?"

Denzel brought his knees closer to his chest and hugged his makeshift pillow tighter. He shouldn't answer. He didn't want to answer. But he knew Smithy wouldn't shut up until he did.

"First one," he said. "And I'd wear an eye patch."

Silence fell. The room was in near total darkness, aside from the faint red glow that King Kong's gemstone emitted. Under any normal circumstances, Denzel would have been pretty excited about sharing a bedroom with the most famous (and arguably only) giant gorilla in the world. Right now, though, he was too tired to even think about it.

"Think we could play baseball tomorrow?" Smithy asked.

"Maybe," Denzel said, without opening his eyes.

"OK, here's another one for you..."

Denzel groaned and rolled on to his back. "No! I don't want to hear it! We need to get to sleep."

"I don't," said Smithy.

Denzel rubbed his eyes and frowned. "What?"

"I don't sleep. I can keep talking all night," Smithy said. Denzel saw him turn and grin in the half-light. "Cool, eh?"

"Maybe you can, but I can't," Denzel reminded him. "I

really need to sleep, Smithy. So, please, just for once..."

The rest of the sentence was lost as Denzel's eyes closed and, bathed in the light of an imprisoned giant gorilla monster, he finally drifted off to sleep.

CHAPTER 11

Denzel awoke with a start. The memory of a nightmare reared up like a monster from the deep, but then quickly retreated, leaving him with just a vague sense of dread.

"What time is it?" he mumbled, addressing the question to the world in general. He looked at his watch, but he hadn't adjusted it to the right time yet, so it didn't help at all.

He was shuffling out of his sleeping bag when he noticed that Smithy was gone. A thin line of light seeped in through the gap under the door, and Denzel thought he could hear voices out there. Martinez, maybe. Smithy, definitely.

The memory of the crushed soldiers leapt back to the forefront of Denzel's half-asleep brain, immediately snapping him all the way awake.

"What have you done?"

That was definitely Martinez's voice.

"Oh no, what now?" Denzel groaned. He finished clambering out of his sleeping bag, then limped towards the door, nursing a pain in his lower back. The floor had been even less comfortable that it had looked, and it had looked *very* uncomfortable.

Denzel nudged open the door to find Smithy sitting at the table. Martinez towered over him, eyes wide, mouth hanging open in surprise.

Between them, all lined up as if ready for an inspection, was an army of undead soldiers.

"I got bored," said Smithy. "I found your glue and paint, and thought I'd try putting some of your guys back together."

Martinez picked up one of the figures – a tiny skeleton with a crossbow – and examined it closely. "You can't even see where it was broken."

He picked up another few of the figures, and scrutinised them closely. "I thought I'd never be able to fix them."

"Nah, it wasn't that difficult," said Smithy. "I mean, I had to shrink down to sort a few of them out, but other than that, it was easy."

"Right, right," said Martinez, still transfixed by his good-as-new figures.

"Wait," said Denzel, stepping fully into the room. "Shrink down? What do you mean?"

"Morning, sleepyhead!" said Smithy.

"Yeah, morning. *Shrink down?* You can shrink down?"

Smithy nodded.

"Since when?"

Smithy's lips moved silently for a moment. He counted quickly on his fingers. "Since eighteen seventy-one," he said. "Well, no, probably since before then, but I found out in eighteen seventy-one. I could hardly believe it. You should've seen my face. Shocked, it was. And tiny. Mostly tiny."

"You never mentioned it before."

"You never asked," said Smithy.

"Why would I ask?" Denzel replied. "I just pretty much assume that people can't change size. What else can you do?"

"Well," said Smithy, rolling the word around in his mouth. "I don't need to sleep."

Denzel picked a lump of gunk from the corner of his eyes and yawned. "Yeah. That one I do know about."

"Thank you," said Martinez. The sincerity of it took

both Smithy and Denzel by surprise. The Oberon reached a hand across the table to Smithy. For the first time since they'd arrived, he didn't look completely terrified of being close to Smithy. "I mean it. Thanks."

"No problem," said Smithy, shaking his hand. "You've got an impressive infantry, although – if you don't mind me saying – you could do with beefing up your archers and mounted division."

Martinez's eyes widened again. "You know about Battlefist?"

Smithy snorted. "Please. I practically invented Battlefist," he said, then he immediately retracted that statement. "OK, that's not even a little bit true, but me and a couple of other ghosts used to play it back in the eighties. I was pretty good at it, if I say so myself."

He shrugged. "OK, that's not even a little bit true either, but I know all the rules. Well, most of them. Well, some of them. Well, I know there's some dice involved, and something about a goblin."

He smiled hopefully. "Why, fancy a game?"

Martinez hesitated, biting his lip. But then he pulled the other chair out from under the table. "Don't mind if I do," he said.

Before they could get any further, the lift door opened. Weinberg emerged. She had an assault rifle that wasn't unlike the one Boyle lugged around with him back home, but this one had a variety of extra bits added on, almost as an afterthought.

She wore a helmet on her head, with a little camera or viewscreen or something positioned over her right eye, and the way she moved suggested she meant business.

"Martinez," she said, her voice sombre and serious. "We've got a problem."

"Is it that smell in the bathroom?" asked Martinez, shuffling a deck of square cards. "I've asked the plumber to come back on Tuesday."

"No. A ghost problem."

Martinez stopped shuffling. His chair creaked as he turned to look at his partner. "What, seriously? Another one?"

"Yup. At the docks," said Weinberg. "Denzel, Smithy, I want you with us."

Smithy jumped to his feet and saluted. "Aye aye, cap'n."

"Uh, sure," said Denzel. "I mean, I should probably go to the toilet first."

"No time. Go when we're there," said Weinberg. She looked him up and down. "But I *would* probably put on some pants if I were you."

Denzel blushed and pulled his T-shirt down to cover

his boxer shorts. "He he. OK," he said, backing towards the kitchen-cum-bedroom-cum-King-Kong-storage area. "Sounds like a plan!"

One long van ride, and what seemed like an even longer walk through a not particularly friendly area later, Denzel and Smithy stood watching Weinberg and Martinez tiptoeing along an old wooden pier.

They'd driven all the way across to the other side of the harbour, and the towering skyscrapers of Manhattan now stood across the bay, gleaming in the morning sunlight. Nothing gleamed in the part of the city they were in now. Graffiti stained the walls of the old buildings around them, most of which seemed to have been long-since abandoned. High chain-link fences had been erected around the whole area, but most of them had been cut open or pushed down, and those that hadn't were brown with rust.

Weinberg hadn't been all that forthcoming with information. The call had come from the contact in the mayor's office again, and had said something about mysterious lights, ghostly moans and "other weirdness". Just what that other weirdness was, or how weird it was, they hadn't been able to say. Or, if they had, Weinberg wasn't sharing it.

"Nice this, innit?" said Smithy.

Denzel hopped from foot to foot, wishing he'd insisted on going to the toilet before they'd left. His bladder felt like it was going to explode, and probably with enough force to take out half the pier.

"Not really," he said.

Smithy looked around. "I've been in worse places."

"Oh? Where?"

"Pretty much the whole of the eighteenth century," Smithy said. "That was a bit grim. This is paradise compared to that."

"That's not really a place though, is it?" said Denzel, jiggling anxiously.

Smithy looked confused.

"It's a time," said Denzel.

Smithy still looked confused.

"Forget it," Denzel said. He spun on the spot to see what was happening with the others. Weinberg and Martinez were still creeping along the pier. Weinberg was crouching low, sweeping with her rifle. Martinez followed behind, his hands raised in case something needed to be zapped or transformed into a frog, or whatever he was planning to do to them.

They were less than a third of the way along the thing, and showing no signs of speeding up. Denzel crossed his legs. "It's no use, I can't hold on," he said. "I need to find somewhere to pee."

"What about there?" said Smithy. He pointed to an old wooden hut with two doors. Above the door on the left, a sign read: "Gents".

"How long have you known that was there?" Denzel yelped, but he didn't bother to wait for an answer. He ran – or as close as he could get with his legs crossed – to the hut and almost sobbed with relief when the door opened with a single shove.

His relief didn't last long. The smell hammered into him, almost sending him crashing back outside. He forced himself to push on through the stink, but it felt like it was pushing back.

The worst of it was coming from an overflowing urinal, which had been blocked with— Actually, he didn't want to know what it had been blocked with.

He pulled the neck of his hoodie over his mouth and tried to breathe through his ears, then diverted into the only one of the four cubicles to still have a door. Using his foot to lift the lid – there was no way he was touching that with his bare hands – Denzel frantically fiddled with his zip.

Finally he took aim and let rip. The sense of relief as his bladder began to empty was immense. It was even worth putting up with the smell for, and there was also the added bonus that he was no longer one unexpected cough away from wetting himself.

He was midway through – far beyond the point of no return – when the water in the toilet began to bubble. At first Denzel thought it was because of the sheer force at which he was peeing into the pan, but the bubbling became too violent for that. It was like a pot of water coming to the boil, and yet the air that rose from within the bowl was cold. Icy cold, in fact, and Denzel saw his breath as he exhaled shakily and tried to race to the finish.

He heard the whispering just as the stream became a dribble. Denzel hurriedly backed away, doing up his trousers as a voice echoed out from within the toilet.

He is coming.

Denzel yelped in fright when he bumped against the door, mistaking it for someone behind him.

He is coming.

Denzel swallowed. His mouth was dry and it took him three attempts to force the words out.

"Wh-who is?" he asked.

And then, with a groaning of pipes and a rattle of porcelain, the toilet exploded.

At least, that was how it seemed to Denzel, but

technically it didn't explode at all. Instead, a towering jet of yellow water erupted straight upwards like a geyser. It slammed against the ceiling, and with the sound of splintering wood ringing in his ears, Denzel pulled open the cubicle door and stumbled out of the hut.

By the time Denzel reached Smithy, the gushing geyser had punched a hole right through the roof. A column of yellow liquid reached several metres into the air, before spraying in all directions like a fountain.

Denzel and Smithy watched it in silence for a few moments.

"Cor," said Smithy at last. "You really *were* bursting, weren't you?"

Weinberg arrived in a clattering of boots. Martinez was still on the pier but had stopped exploring and was standing watching the urine fountain.

"What happened?" asked Weinberg. "Did you do that?"

"Well, I mean ... I was there when it happened," said Denzel. "But I don't really think it was my fault or anything. There was this voice from the toilet and then *kersploosh*."

Smithy nodded. "You did a poo."

"What? No! I mean *that* happened." Denzel gestured to the roof of the hut. The water was still gushing up from the toilets below.

"A voice?" said Weinberg. "What kind of voice? What did it say?"

"It said, 'He is coming.'"

Weinberg raised her eyebrows, clearly expecting more. "Who is coming?" she asked, when it became clear Denzel wasn't going to continue.

Denzel shrugged. "I don't know. I didn't hang about to ask. But I heard the same thing at the swimming pool." He gasped. "And, yesterday, last night, whenever it was, the guy on the door said the same thing as I got into the lift."

"Harvey?" said Weinberg.

"Yes! 'He is coming.' That's what he said too, but then there was all the stuff with the pizza and Martinez's soldiers and it went completely out of my head." Denzel looked back at the column of water. "What do you think it means?"

"That some bloke's coming?" Smithy guessed.

Weinberg hesitated, but then shrugged. "It's probably nothing," she said.

A sudden flash from behind made Denzel, Weinberg and Smithy turn. They caught a brief glimpse of the water in the harbour being illuminated by a piercing white light, then it quickly returned to its normal choppy darkness.

"Was that underwater lightning?" Denzel asked.

"I have no idea," Weinberg admitted. She cupped her hands around her eyes to block out the sun and looked along the pier to where Martinez was tentatively leaning over the edge, gazing down into the water lapping at the wooden struts below.

The walkie-talkie on Weinberg's belt crackled into life. "Uh, Weinberg?" said Martinez. "It could be my imagination but I think there's something down there. Over."

"Is it dolphins?" asked Smithy. He nudged Weinberg with an elbow. "Ask him if it's dolphins."

"Spectral? Over," said Weinberg, skilfully managing to completely ignore what Smithy had said.

"I think so," said Martinez. "We're going to have to check it out. Over."

"Copy that," said Weinberg. She hooked the radio back on her belt, clapped her gloved hands together once, then smiled broadly at Denzel and Smithy. "So," she began, switching her gaze between them. "How are you guys at swimming?"

CHAPTER 12

It took almost three hours to get back to the Empire State Building, collect the equipment they needed, then return to the docks.

The toilet geyser had stopped spraying, and the hut now stood still and silent, albeit with a few streams of yellow liquid trickling down the walls and pooling on the concrete slabs below.

Weinberg had been able to find a way past the fences and other barricades, and bring the van right up to the edge of the pier. It was just as well, because the equipment they'd picked up back at base was pretty heavy. Ridiculously heavy, in fact. Denzel could barely carry it, so he had no idea how he was supposed to swim in it.

He slapped along the pier in a pair of oversized flippers, his rubber wetsuit chafing him in places he'd really rather not be chafed. Which was everywhere, basically.

Martinez walked ahead, chanting below his breath, the equipment levitating along beside him. Behind him, Weinberg waddled along in her own wetsuit-and-flippers combo, while Smithy trotted along at Denzel's back. Both Smithy and Martinez were dressed normally. If you didn't count Martinez's robe, golden belt and pointy shoes, that is.

"So tell me again," said Denzel. "Why is it just us two?"

"Because you're the one who's been hearing voices," said Weinberg. "If whatever's down there is connected to the 'He is coming' stuff, then I want you there to tell me if you hear anything. Plus, either me or Martinez need to stay up here and keep a lookout, in case anything goes wrong."

"Wrong?" Denzel spluttered. "What do you mean? What could go wrong?"

"Well—" Smithy began, but Denzel stopped him going any further.

"OK, OK! Now I come to think about it, I don't actually want to know!"

"Probably for the best," Weinberg mumbled.

"What?!"

"Hmm? Oh, nothing," said Weinberg. "This'll do, Martinez."

The words Martinez had been muttering changed, and the equipment turned in the air. Denzel took a worried step back as one of the things floated towards him. Weinberg had called it a "Subsea Suit" but if it was a suit, then there was quite a lot of it missing.

Essentially, it was a glass dome with a couple of shoulder pads, a chest plate and some padded arms with gloves on the end. Two short vents extended from the back of the shoulders, and Denzel couldn't help but notice that one of his was held on by tape.

"Relax. It's perfectly safe," said Weinberg. "I built it myself."

That didn't exactly fill Denzel with confidence, but he thought it best not to say as much. Instead, he planted his feet and braced himself as the Subsea Suit slid over his head and down on to his shoulder.

The sounds of the city became distant and echoey, and were replaced by the sound of Denzel's own breathing as the glass dome locked in place over his head. A cool breeze filtered in from somewhere above him, tickling his scalp. Weinberg had warned him that would happen, and assured him the whole thing was watertight. The suit held enough air to last almost ninety minutes, and a tiny hidden pump would keep it circulating throughout their trip.

Denzel started to walk forwards but the weight of the suit pulled him back. He would have toppled over had it not been for Martinez stepping behind him and catching him by the shoulders.

"You OK?" Martinez asked. His voice sounded muffled and far away. Denzel shouted back to make himself heard, and the boom of his voice almost made his eardrums pop.

"Fine! Terrified, but fine!"

There was a soft hiss from somewhere near his ear, like a snake getting ready to strike, before Weinberg's voice replaced it. "You receiving me, Denzel?"

"Uh, yes. Over," said Denzel.

"It's two way; you don't need to say 'over'," Weinberg told him.

"Oh. OK. Over," said Denzel. "I mean, not over. I mean OK."

Weinberg had given him a quick introduction to the Subsea Suit during the drive over. There were two joysticks built into the palms of the gloves, which controlled direction, and a button that acted as the throttle. If he'd ever played Minecraft, she'd said, he'd be able to master it in no time.

Unfortunately, Denzel had only played Minecraft once, six months ago, and something about the way everything had spun around on screen had made him vomit into one of his shoes. Still, he was sure he'd get the hang of it. Eventually.

"You know who you look like?" Smithy asked.

Denzel shrugged. Or he tried to, but couldn't. "Darth Vader?" he guessed. Smithy shook his head. "C3PO? A Dalek? A Cyberman? Someone else out of *Doctor Who*?"

Smithy kept shaking his head. "Give up?" he asked eventually.

"I give up. Who do I look like?"

Smithy pointed to Weinberg. "Her," he said. "It's probably the diving-suit thing."

Denzel searched Smithy's face for any sign he was winding him up but saw nothing to suggest he was. "Yeah, it's probably that," he agreed, then he followed Weinberg to the edge of the wooden platform.

The water looked almost completely black. It lurked beneath them like a vast, endless cavern, just waiting to swallow them whole.

"I'd say the source of the light is maybe sixty feet that way," said Martinez, pointing away from the shore. "But deep. Way down deep."

"Gotcha," said Weinberg, and Denzel heard her voice through the glass and the speaker inside his helmet at the same time. "Ready, Denzel?"

"Not really," Denzel admitted. He wondered if it was too late to go to the toilet again, but then Weinberg's hand was on his back and, with a shove from her, he tumbled over the edge and plunged into the icy blackness of the Hudson River.

A current tugged on Denzel's flippers, pulling him deeper beneath the surface. A spotlight illuminated on top of the suit's domed helmet, cutting a thin beam through the murky water.

The Hudson River, Smithy had helpfully told him, after googling it on one of Weinberg's many laptops she seemed to just leave lying around in the back of the van, was one of the most polluted rivers in the whole of the United States. Factories had been pumping waste into the water for decades, so many of the things living down there had been killed off. Those creatures that hadn't died off had become larger, tougher and probably quite a lot angrier – and that was round about the time Denzel had closed the lid of the laptop and hastily changed the subject.

Through the gloom, Denzel saw another light

illuminate. Weinberg. At least, he hoped so. It was either her or one of those ugly fish with the lights on their head and all the teeth. If it was one of them, he reckoned, and it came swimming out of the dark at him, there was a very good chance he'd immediately die of fright.

"Hey, Denzel. You OK?"

"Uh. Yes. Ish," said Denzel. "Is that you? The light, I mean?"

The light bobbed up and down. "Yeah, that's me," said Weinberg. "Suit OK? Any leaks?"

"Leaks?" Denzel yelped. "No! I mean, I don't think so! Why are you asking that? Why would there be leaks?"

He tried to turn his head to check the back of the helmet, but only succeeded in turning himself the whole way around. He couldn't feel any water seeping through though. If there had been a leak, he'd have noticed by now, wouldn't he?

It wasn't as cold as he'd imagined. There had been a brief biting chill when he'd first hit the water, but it had passed in a few seconds, and now it was surprisingly ... not comfortable, that was too far. Tolerable, maybe.

"It's darker than I expected," said Weinberg.

"Do you know where we're going?" Denzel asked.

A light pulsed some distance away. It was brief and bright, and came from somewhere deep beneath them.

"That way, I guess," said Weinberg.

Denzel squeezed the throttle buttons in his gloves. Tiny motors inside the suit *whirred* and he shot forwards, throwing out two trails of bubbles behind him.

With propellers spinning and flippers kicking, Denzel and Weinberg swam onwards into the dark.

CHAPTER 13

The floor of the Hudson was dotted with all sorts of random junk. Denzel's light picked out the skeletons of old shopping trolleys, sunken boats, rusty barrels and even what looked like part of a plane.

There were surprisingly few fish, which he was pretty pleased about. Fish freaked him out, if he were honest, even the ones without the lights on their head. He'd had visions of being surrounded by the things, but they'd only spotted a handful, and they'd all quickly scarpered when they'd seen Weinberg and Denzel approaching.

"Martinez hates the water," said Weinberg. "That's the main reason for leaving him up there. I just didn't want to say it in front of him."

"Oh," said Denzel. "Right. I mean, I'm not exactly water's biggest fan either…"

Weinberg laughed. "Trust me, you're already doing waaaaay better than he would be. If it hadn't been for you guys being there, I doubt he'd even have set foot on the pier."

"He seems to be frightened of a lot of stuff," Denzel said.

"Yeah, maybe," Weinberg conceded. "But he can pull it together when it counts."

They swam on for another couple of minutes, heading roughly in the direction they thought the flash had come from. Weinberg had explained the suits had some built-in scanning equipment but hadn't told Denzel how any of it operated. He was relieved, actually. It was taking all his concentration just to keep on top of the steering.

"I'm not picking up any Spectral Energy," Weinberg said. "Maybe a little background stuff, but nothing you wouldn't expect. Less than you'd expect, even."

Denzel said nothing. He had no idea how much Spectral Energy he should expect down here. He wasn't even sure how Spectral Energy was measured. In per cent? Millilitres? Marks out of ten?

"It's barely hitting four Gloogs," Weinberg said.

Ah. Gloogs. Of course, thought Denzel. *Because that isn't ridiculous at all.*

"That's not a lot of Gloogs," he said, even though he had no idea how many Gloogs would be considered a reasonable number. Or, in fact, what a Gloog even was.

Denzel felt a tingling beneath his wetsuit, like a low hum of electricity across his skin. The water around him grew colder.

"Did you feel that?" he asked.

"Feel what?"

The light came again, a sudden blinding flash from dead ahead. Denzel heard Weinberg hiss, and found himself doing the same as the light pushed down on his eyes like thumbs, forcing him to screw them shut and turn his head.

Even with his eyes closed, the halo of white still lingered. There was something else too – a dark outline right at the centre of the light. A tall, chunky rectangle that looked remarkably like...

"A door," said Weinberg, her voice coming through the speaker as a hushed whisper. "There's a door."

Denzel opened his eyes and blinked a few times, trying to clear the dazzling spots that clouded his vision.

Weinberg was right. There was a door. An enormous stone frame was picked out in the beam of Denzel's torch. He leaned back, trying to figure out how tall it was. He could see maybe ten metres of it, straight up, but everything beyond that was hidden by the murk.

Symbols were carved into each of the roughly hewn bricks that made up the frame. Some of them were simple enough – an X, an angular P, something that looked like an arrow – but others were ornate swirls and curves he'd never seen before. Something about them gave him the heebie-jeebies though, and he steered himself closer to Weinberg, just to be on the safe side.

Her light shone on the door itself. It was made of a dark-grey wood and covered in the most elaborate carvings Denzel had ever seen. There were more symbols here, but other things too – snakes and dragons and sea serpents all writhing and entwining around each other; swords and axes, locked together as if in battle.

But it was the face that troubled Denzel the most. It was carved near the bottom of the door, roughly at what would be head-height for a tall adult, were they standing on the riverbed itself. It had chiselled cheeks, two etched lines to suggest closed eyes, and a roughly hewn wooden beard. While it was obviously just a carving, there was something eerily realistic about it at the same time, and Denzel swam upwards a little so his light was no longer shining directly on it.

In among all the carved shapes was a series of large metal studs. They ran at regular intervals up the length of the door, and dozens of much smaller symbols and icons had been etched on to each one

"What is it?" Denzel whispered.

"A door."

Denzel tutted. "Well, I mean, yes. I can see that. But what's it doing here?"

"I have no idea," Weinberg admitted. She set off swimming along the front of the door, and Denzel hurried to follow.

They swam for what felt like quite a long time. Just as Denzel was sure the door must be about to come to an end, Weinberg's light revealed a second door butted right up against it. They continued swimming on, eventually reaching the other edge of the stone frame after a good two more minutes.

They'd passed several more of the faces along the way, each one similar, but different. They all had beards, they all had their eyes closed, but the shapes of the heads were never quite the same. Denzel had hurried past them all, never letting his light linger.

"OK, so it's not just one door, it's a double set," said Weinberg. "And it's big. Like, really big."

She steered herself around the side of the doorframe.

For a moment, all Denzel could see were the bubbles from her Subsea Suit's propellers, then she swam back into view.

"Nothing behind it. It's just a door. Just a massive door at the bottom of the Hudson River, which occasionally emits blinding flashes of white light."

Denzel nodded. That seemed to pretty much sum it up. He might have added "creepy" before the word "massive", and possibly underlined it for emphasis, but it was a pretty accurate description all the same.

"Any ideas?" Weinberg asked.

Denzel puffed out his cheeks. "Swim away and nuke it from orbit?" he said. It really was *very* creepy.

"What are you talking about?" Weinberg said. She laughed, which, to Denzel, seemed highly inappropriate, given the circumstances. "This could be the find of … well, not the century. There was that demon portal in France a couple of years back. But, you know, it could be a pretty major find we're looking at here. We need to examine this thing."

Denzel was about to ask if they could examine it from very far away – ideally another country – when his skin began to tingle. The temperature of the water dropped rapidly. Even inside the glass helmet, Denzel saw his breath become white vapour.

"Look out!" he warned, but then the light hit them. Denzel closed his eyes and tried to turn away, but the brightness of the flash was overwhelming. He and Weinberg both cried out in pain and shock, spinning in the water as they tried to shield themselves from the glare.

Like before, the flash only lasted for a fraction of a second, but up close it was even more disorientating. Denzel turned, flailing out. His helmet hit the door with a *thud*. He stopped moving and held his breath, terrified he was going to hear the glass crack and feel water come flooding in.

Luckily, he didn't. Denzel blinked away the light spots again and placed a hand on the door to push himself clear.

Even through the glove, he felt the vibration as he touched the wood. The carved symbol closest to his hand illuminated in a fiery orange glow. Another symbol just a little further above his hand lit up next. Then two on the left. Then one below.

He yanked his hand free and watched with a growing sense of dread as the carved symbols continued to illuminate all across the wood, spreading out from the spot where he had touched it. He glanced sideways at Weinberg, but she was still facing the other way, trying to recover from being dazzled.

"Um…" said Denzel, which was pretty much the best he could come up with at the moment. "Um…"

The tiny etchings on the metal studs were starting to light up now. Through the murk, Denzel could see other spots of orange appear, as every one of the door's symbols flickered into life.

"Wow, that was bright," said Weinberg. "You OK?"

"Not really," Denzel said.

Weinberg turned and let out a little gasp when she saw the door. It was ablaze with colour now, the light dancing and flickering, as if flames were burning behind each symbol.

"This isn't good, is it?" Denzel whispered.

"I don't know," Weinberg admitted. "I mean, you know, probably not for *us*…"

The face nearest to Denzel flicked open its eyes so suddenly that Denzel would swear he lost three years off his life expectancy through sheer terror alone. The eyes, which were also carved, although much more skilfully than the rest of the face, turned to look at Denzel.

"N-no, definitely not good," Denzel whispered, and then the wooden face snapped open its mouth, spewing a jet of fast-moving bubbles towards Denzel and Weinberg. The bubbles shoved them both backwards away from the doorframe.

Several other churning streams of bubbles appeared further along the door. Denzel imagined all those other faces, eyes and mouths now open, screaming silently in the darkness.

From somewhere on the other side of the wood, there was a loud *kalunk* that seemed to echo through the water.

And then slowly, ever so slowly, the doors began to open.

CHAPTER 14

What emerged through the opening was … nothing at all. The doors parted, revealing the patch of water directly behind it, a couple of startled-looking fish and not a whole lot else.

"Well, that's an anti-climax," Weinberg said. "Huh. Looks like it's nothing to worry about."

Denzel was about to point out that she probably shouldn't tempt fate like that, when the space in the centre of the doorway began to glow an eerie shade of green.

The light quickly became a thrashing, churning, heaving mass of glowing bubbles that whipped the water around them into a frenzied spinning whirlpool.

"You had to say it, didn't you?" yelped Denzel. "You just had to say it."

"Uh, we should probably go," said Weinberg, steering herself around in her Subsea Suit and firing up the propellers.

"You think?" Denzel said, kicking frantically with his flippers as he squeezed on the throttle buttons.

"Going to open channel. Martinez!" Weinberg said, and suddenly Martinez's voice was echoing around in Denzel's fishbowl-like helmet.

"Martinez here. What's going on?"

"Nothing good," said Weinberg. "We're returning to the surface. Get ready with—"

A gush of bubbles *whooshed* past Denzel from behind, catching him in their slipstream and dragging him through the water. He spun out of control, his light swinging wildly through the dark water as he flipped and rolled on the sudden current.

"Weinberg, help!" he called, but the only reply was the sound of bubbling water that was all around him now, hurtling him onwards.

WHUMP!

One of Denzel's shoulders slammed into a piece of

debris, sending a shockwave of pain crashing through him.

The impact spun him out of the path of the bubble torrent and he hit the riverbed hard, churning the sediment up into thick brown clouds around him. The head-mounted torch flickered twice, then went off. Denzel managed to stretch the arms of the suit above his head until he found the light. He hit it a few times, then sighed with relief when the light returned.

"Weinberg. I'm OK," he said.

Silence.

"Hey, Weinberg," said Denzel, his tightening throat turning his voice into a croak. "You there?"

No response.

"Martinez?"

Nothing.

"Oh good," Denzel whispered. "Either my radio got knocked out or everyone's dead."

He realised the bubbles had stopped. The water was silent again. Too silent, almost. Other than the echo of his own breathing, Denzel could hear nothing at all.

Still, he was alive and in one piece, so things weren't all bad. He gave the joysticks in his gloves a try and the Subsea Suit *whirred* into life. No damage there either then. In many ways, he'd actually had a pretty lucky escape.

Krick.

Denzel's eyes crossed as he watched a tiny hairline crack appear in the glass of his helmet. He swallowed. "Oh, come *on*," he whispered.

Krick.

Denzel kicked off from the floor of the Hudson, churning the silt and dirt around as he launched himself towards the surface, squeezing both throttle triggers for dear life. The Subsea Suit propelled him upwards through the water. As he rose towards the surface, the all-consuming blackness lightened, gradually becoming a deep, brooding shade of green.

Krick.

The crack grew. Condensation suddenly bloomed on the inside of the glass, making it impossible for Denzel to see anything beyond it. He had no idea how far away the surface was, or even if he was still heading in the right direction. He gritted his teeth and kicked, then watched in horror as a single drip of dirty river water found its way inside the helmet.

"Ooh, not good," Denzel hissed. He squeezed the throttle triggers with such force his hands began to shake. His flippers swished behind him. The surface had to be up there somewhere. Didn't it?!

The helmet splintered into a spider's-web pattern, and Denzel felt moisture on his face. He drew in a breath, terrified that the dome was about to give way completely. The water around him was a forest green now, even through the cracked and misted visor. *How much further? How much—*

He broke the surface and let out a sharp yelp of relief as the water stopped trying to force its way inside the suit. The condensation lining the inside of the helmet began to fade, and Denzel looked around in confusion, trying to figure out where he'd come up.

The pier was twelve metres or so away, but barely visible through a weird green fog that hung over the water. Denzel steered himself towards the wooden platform. It wasn't until he was much closer that he saw the figures standing on the pier. They were calling his name, but their voices were muffled, either by the glass or by the fog.

"Hey!" said Denzel, grabbing for the pier edge. Above him, Smithy screamed in panic, raised a leg, then brought a foot slamming down on to Denzel's helmet. Another spider's-web pattern appeared in the glass, and Denzel cried out, "Smithy, stop, it's me!"

"Whoops!" said Smithy. "Sorry, thought you were a big jellyfish."

"Oh, Denzel, thank God," said Weinberg. She was still in her rubber diving gear, but had removed her Subsea Suit. "When I lost contact with you, I thought—" She stopped talking and just smiled instead. "I'm glad you're OK."

She and Smithy both bent down and helped haul Denzel up on to the pier. He flopped on to his back, then groaned with relief when Weinberg unclipped his helmet and pulled him free of the suit.

Out of the helmet, the fog seemed even thicker somehow. It wasn't just above the water; it stretched out towards the shore too. The hut with the exploding toilet wasn't far away, Denzel knew, but it was currently lost somewhere in the rolling green mist.

"What's going on?" Denzel asked as he got to his feet. His voice sounded flat and lifeless in the fog, and seemed to bounce back to him from every direction at once. "What is this stuff?"

"Fog," said Smithy.

"But it's green."

Smithy nodded. "All fog's green."

"No, it isn't."

Smithy frowned. "Isn't it? Well, what am I thinking of then?"

"Spectral readings are off the charts," said Weinberg.

This didn't really come as a surprise, even to Denzel. The fog definitely had a certain ghostly feel to it, and his skin was prickling in a way that told him danger of the supernatural variety was close, and probably getting closer.

"We should get back to base," said Martinez, his eyes darting anxiously down at the water. "You can run some tests. I know a few divinations that might help us figure this out. We shouldn't be out here."

Denzel wasn't going to argue with that. Being inside felt much safer than being outside at the moment. Also, he kind of needed the toilet again, and he had no idea how to get his wetsuit off.

"Agreed," said Weinberg. She set off along the pier. "Let's get back to the van and find out how far this fog goes."

"What about the suits?" asked Denzel, gesturing to his own discarded diving equipment. "Shouldn't we take them?"

"We can come back," said Martinez, ushering Denzel and Smithy on. "Right now, we need to get out of here, in case..."

Denzel and Smithy hurried on, closing the gap on Weinberg. It was only when they'd run several metres that Denzel realised Martinez had stopped talking. He turned back and saw the Oberon boy through the fog, his fingers dancing lightly in the air.

"What is it? What's the matter?" Denzel asked. "Why have you stopped?"

"There's something out there," said Martinez, the mist making his voice thin and reedy. "Something in the fog. Or in the water. Something—"

A shape – huge and grey – flashed in the fog behind Martinez, moving quickly towards him. Denzel caught a glimpse of a glistening black circle, a blood-red gum and the biggest teeth he'd ever seen.

And then the shape and Martinez were gone.

"Uh, Denzel," said Smithy, appearing beside him.

"Y-yes?"

"This might be a silly question."

"G-go for it."

"Promise you won't laugh?"

Denzel nodded slowly, not taking his eyes off the spot where Martinez had been standing.

"OK," said Smithy. "Here goes. Did Martinez just get eaten by a big monster?"

Denzel swallowed. "Pretty much," he said hoarsely.

They both looked down as the pier began to shake. Through the mist, they heard the sound of wood splintering. Denzel felt his stomach drop down somewhere around his toes as, ahead of them, the pier began to disintegrate.

There, slicing through the wood towards them, taller than Denzel and Smithy put together, was a shark's fin.

Denzel and Smithy turned to look at each other. "We're probably not going to get that game of baseball today, are we?" said Smithy.

Denzel shook his head.

"What you think?" said Smithy. "Run?"

"Yeah," Denzel whispered. "I think probably run."

They turned and hurtled, side by side, through the fog, the pier shuddering beneath them as the fin tore along it like an industrial saw. Neither of them stopped when they reached solid ground, and it wasn't until they almost knocked Weinberg off her feet that they dared slow down.

"Watch it!" she said. She looked back in the direction they'd come. "Where's Martinez?"

Denzel opened his mouth, but only a squeak emerged. He gulped down a breath and tried again. "Shark."

"Big shark," Smithy added. He too seemed to be having trouble breathing, despite the fact he didn't actually need to. He stretched his arms out to convey just how big the shark was, but it didn't really do it justice.

"What do you mean? Where's Martinez?" Weinberg

demanded, but Denzel quickly clamped a hand over her mouth.

A vast shape had appeared from the fog over in the direction of the pier. It slunk through the air, as if swimming through the mist itself.

They could only see part of the outline, but what they *could* see was the size of a double-decker bus. It twitched as it flicked its tail, propelling itself around in a lazy, swooping arc that would, sooner or later, lead it directly to them.

"Is that the big shark?" Smithy whispered.

"I think so," said Denzel.

"Shouldn't it be in the water?" asked Smithy.

"Again, I think so," said Denzel.

"Should we maybe, I don't know, tell it?"

"Probably not," Denzel whispered.

He slowly moved his hand away from Weinberg's mouth. She swallowed, her eyes fixed on the shape in the fog. "Get in the van," she said. "Quietly."

Smithy nodded and took hold of the handles that opened the van's back doors. "No, wait!" Weinberg said, fumbling for her keys.

Too late! Smithy pulled on the handles and the van's horn began to blare out. All its lights flashed at once as the alarm sounded, and the shape in the fog jerked suddenly towards them.

Smithy grinned nervously. "Uh, the van's making a noise. Why is the van making a noise? Should the van be making that noise?"

There was a series of *clunks* as all the van's many locks released. "Shut up and get in!" Weinberg yelped, pulling open the driver's door and clambering inside.

Smithy and Denzel each yanked open one of the back doors. They scrambled inside just as the engine roared into life, and Denzel almost tumbled out when the van lurched forwards. A vision of black eyes and enormous teeth spurred his legs into action, and he kicked himself along the van's smooth floor until Smithy caught him by the arm.

The alarm was still blasting out. The flashing lights illuminated the green fog, giving Denzel and Smithy a brief glimpse of the shark's scarred and pock-marked snout, before Weinberg barged through a fence, skidded on to a side street and floored the accelerator.

For a long time, Denzel and Smithy didn't speak. It was Smithy who eventually broke the silence.

"I think we're gonna need a bigger van."

CHAPTER 15

The van skidded on to another street, making the open back doors flap around. The fog was as thick as ever, but Denzel could still see the outline of the shark chasing them down. It was faster on the straights than they were, but slower on the turns. Weinberg slammed the vehicle into a sideways skid and on to another side road, to try to buy them some more time.

"Weapons!" she called back over her shoulder. "In the crates."

Denzel and Smithy both looked around for crates, then realised they were sitting on them. Denzel yanked open the lid of the box he'd been perched on. There was something that looked worryingly like a child's ray-gun toy, a pair of chain-mail gloves with little screens mounted on each wrist, and something that looked like a radio-controlled drone.

Denzel glanced outside at the house-sized monster shark chasing them, then reluctantly picked up the tiny ray gun.

"Here, Denzel, what would you rather, right?" Smithy asked.

Denzel shook his head. "Not now, Smithy."

"No, but—"

"I said *not now*, Smithy! Big shark. Currently chasing us. Remember?"

Denzel took aim with his gun. He squeezed the trigger. The gun made a sort of *bloop* sound and a tiny red pellet flew five metres, then dropped to the ground and vanished into the fog.

"Well, that's just great," said Denzel, then he yelped as a stream of crackling energy erupted from right behind him, punched a hole in the mist and struck the shark right on its snout. The monster banked sharply right, smashed into a row of parked cars, which all flipped over, then rejoined the chase.

Denzel turned to find Smithy holding a device that was roughly the length of a golf umbrella. Plastic tubes ran along the sides of it, with colourful liquid burbling inside each one. Something a bit like a funnel was attached to the end. "Like I was saying," said Smithy. "What would you rather, right? That tiny ray gun of yours?" He gestured down to a second umbrella-sized device on the floor between them. "Or one of *these*?"

"What is it?" Denzel asked.

"They're Dephantomisers," Weinberg shouted from the front seat, twisting the wheel to avoid an abandoned car that appeared in the fog ahead.

"What's a Dephantomiser when it's at home?" Denzel wondered.

Smithy shrugged. "Dunno," he admitted, then he grinned. "But I have a feeling it's going to be fun to find out."

Snatching the device up, Denzel rested the butt of it against his hip. "OK," he said, "how do I make it—"

The liquid in the tubes *burbled* and a blast of energy spat from the end of the weapon, just as one of the doors flapped closed. The door exploded outwards with a *screech* of twisting metal. It tumbled off through the fog, and seemed to pass straight through the chasing shark. Either that, or the shark ate it. It was hard to be sure, from that distance.

Denzel jumped in fright, arcing the blast upwards. It

carved a half-metre-long slice through the roof before Denzel had the sense to take his finger off the trigger. Breathing heavily, and trembling slightly, he turned to find Smithy watching him.

"Yeah," said Smithy. "Like that."

"What the hell are you doing?" Weinberg demanded. She spun the wheel and Denzel was slammed into the side of the van, then Smithy was slammed into the side of Denzel. Denzel's weapon went off again. A rainbow-coloured beam of energy punched through the empty passenger seat up front, and the windscreen exploded out of its frame.

"Argh! Be careful!" Weinberg screamed.

"Sorry!" said Denzel.

He and Smithy tucked themselves in between the seats and the crates. Weinberg's driving was throwing them around all over the place, and Denzel hoped the heavy boxes would stop him and Smithy falling out next time she skidded around a corner.

They both rested their elbows on the crate lids and took aim with the Dephantomisers. The shark was speeding through the fog towards them. It was too wide for the street, but its ghostly body passed effortlessly through the buildings on either side. Most of the time, at least. Occasionally, usually on a bend, it would slam into a building, or knock over a street light, or nudge aside cars, but then it would become like vapour again, and go back to phasing through everything in its path.

"What will you give me if I can hit it in the eye?" Smithy asked.

"A million dollars," said Denzel.

Smithy's head turned sharply. "Seriously?"

"No," said Denzel. "I'll give you … some enthusiastic applause. How about that?"

"Deal," said Smithy. He squeezed the trigger. Energy crackled. A parked motorbike exploded, taking out two other bikes on either side.

"This time," said Smithy. He opened fire again. A delivery truck went up in flames.

"No, wait, *this* time."

A street light was sliced in two.

"*This* time."

A fire hydrant erupted, spraying water into the sky.

"Just stop shooting!" said Denzel. "There'll be nothing of the city left."

Smithy leaned back from the gun's sights. "Oh, wait, hang on. I had the wrong eye closed," he said. "OK, *definitely* this time."

He took aim at the oncoming shark. He squeezed the trigger, just as Weinberg sent the van into a spinning skid.

The energy blast tore across the entire bottom floor of a derelict dockside building. Bricks and boarded-up windows disintegrated. Denzel and Smithy both watched, eyes wide, mouths hanging open, as the whole building shifted on its unstable base and began to topple.

"F-faster!" Denzel yelped.

Weinberg gripped the wheel. "Is the shark catching up?"

Denzel swallowed. "If by 'shark' you mean 'eight-storey building', then yes."

"That wasn't my fault," Smithy insisted, but then anything else he said was drowned out by the sound of an eight-storey building becoming a one-storey pile of rubble. It was, Denzel reckoned, one of the loudest things he'd ever heard. It was like a load of explosions had got together and were all trying to outdo one another.

Dust and smoke billowed into the air and rolled along the street after the speeding van, mingling with the green fog. Several car alarms screamed, then were suddenly silenced as debris smashed down on the vehicles, covering them completely.

"Can you see it?" Weinberg shouted.

"Yeah, it's all over the road," said Smithy. "But, again, totally not my fault."

"Not the building, the shark!"

Smithy frowned for a moment, then raised his eyebrows high. "Oh. Haha. I completely forgot about that."

"We're almost at the Brooklyn Bridge," Weinberg announced, although that didn't really mean much to Denzel or Smithy.

"Great!" Denzel said. He wasn't sure if it *was* great or not, but he felt he should probably say something.

He peered through the mist and the dust. The mound of rubble was only just visible now, and fading rapidly. The shark, however, was nowhere to be seen. Could the falling building have stopped it? Was the shark pinned under all that debris, unable to get free?

"Can't see it," Denzel said. "I think it might be—"

"Brace, brace, brace!" Weinberg screamed.

The shark emerged from a side street and drove its snout into the side of the van, sending the vehicle into a violent roll. Denzel and Smithy hit the ceiling, then the floor, then the walls, tumbling around as the van flipped across the tarmac.

There was a sudden *bang* that flung them against the back of the seats, and then they dropped on to the ceiling, which – for reasons Denzel was too dazed to figure out – was beneath them.

"Denzel?" said Smithy. He, unlike Denzel and Weinberg, was completely unhurt. One of the many advantages of being a ghost was that it was very difficult to actually be harmed, on account of already being dead.

Denzel groaned and fluttered open his eyelids. His whole body ached, but it was a sort of "warning ache" that suggested much worse was going to come in the next few minutes, once his brain had fully taken stock of the damage.

The first thing Denzel saw was Smithy's face, leaning sideways into his field of vision with an expression of concern.

The second thing he saw was the shark. It approached slowly through the fog, its tail flicking lazily, like it knew its prey was no longer going anywhere.

"The Dephantomisers?" Denzel managed to wheeze.

"I think they fell out," Smithy told him.

With a groan of effort, Denzel managed to raise himself on to his knees. Glass crunched under him as he struggled on to his feet.

"Guys, you need to go," Weinberg coughed. She was still in her chair, hanging upside down. There was a cut on her head, and a bruise already starting to bloom on her chin. She hissed in pain as she pulled her virtual-reality-style headset over her eyes.

"We'll get you out," Denzel told her.

"No time," said Weinberg. She adjusted a dial on the side of the visor. "Hold on to your—"

Denzel felt a sensation like he was suddenly falling. He looked down, but where there should have been the van ceiling, he saw only blackness. His feet stretched out, swirling into tiny specks, as if his entire body were being reduced to ash.

No, not ash, he realised. Atoms.

And then, with a *thump*, Denzel and Smithy landed on the discarded pizza boxes back in the Empire State Building headquarters.

Grabbing the table, Denzel heaved himself back to his feet. The room was in near darkness, aside from the eerie red glow of Kong's gemstone.

"Weinberg?" Denzel yelped. He spun on the spot, looking upwards in the hope of seeing the Vulteron girl come plunging out of thin air, just like they had. No such luck. She hadn't followed them, which meant...

Actually, Denzel didn't want to think about what it meant. The shark had been close. Weinberg had been stuck in her seat, the van's doors crushing in around her.

"What do we do?" Denzel asked, turning to Smithy. He found him halfway through a slice of day-old pizza. "Ugh! What are you doing?"

"Eating," said Smithy. "Shame to let it go to waste."

Denzel grabbed Smithy by the arm and pulled him towards the door. "Come on, we need to go back for her, or get help, or ... something!"

Throwing open the door, Denzel barged through into the larger basement area, then gasped when he saw a figure lurking in the shadows. With a yelp of fright, he ducked, dragging Smithy with him, just as a bolt of sizzling energy streaked across the room and hit the doorframe with a *bang* and a flash of blinding white.

CHAPTER 16

"Whoa, whoa, whoa, Martinez, stop! It's us!" Denzel cried.

Across the room, Martinez stepped from the shadows. He kept his hands raised, like he might fire off another bolt of magic at any second. They were shaking, Denzel noticed, and his face was almost as pale as Smithy's.

"D-Denzel?"

Smithy leaned out from behind Denzel's back. "And me," he said, taking another bite of the stale pizza base. "Hang on. Weren't you eaten by a massive shark?"

Martinez shook his head slowly. "Recall spell," he said. "Brought me back here." He peered past them, into the

King Kong storage room. "Where's Weinberg?"

"We, uh, we don't know," Denzel admitted. "The van, it was flipped, and then she teleported us here. We need to go and help her."

"Are you nuts?" Martinez gasped. "We can't go back out there."

Denzel blinked in surprise. "What? But Weinberg's out there somewhere. She needs our help."

"Also, massive ghost shark," said Smithy. "Which is probably part of your job description."

"We can't just leave her out there. We can't just leave *anyone* out there with that thing," Denzel protested.

"Oh, and what do you suggest we do, huh?" said Martinez, finally lowering his hands. "How do you suggest we fix this?"

"Well, I mean, I don't know, do I?" said Denzel. "You're the experienced one. We're just... Well, I don't know what we are, exactly."

"Loveable idiots," said Smithy.

Denzel hesitated. "Well, I was going to say 'trainees'."

Martinez laughed. It was a dry, hoarse sort of laugh with zero humour in it. "'Experienced'. Me? You think?" he said. "You know how many ghosts – actual real, genuine ghosts – I've seen since finishing training?"

"Three hundred and six," Smithy guessed. "Wait, no.

Three hundred and *seven*."

"One," said Martinez. "One. And do you know how many of those *weren't* a giant ghost shark? None."

Denzel did the maths in his head. It took him a little longer than usual but he put that down to the number of knocks his skull had recently taken.

"So that was the first ghost you've ever seen?!" he said. "Seriously?"

"Yep."

Denzel jabbed a thumb back in Smithy's direction. They both raised their eyebrows.

"What? Oh. Yes. Well ... he doesn't count." Martinez said.

"Yes I do!" said Smithy. "I'll give you that I struggle with multiplication, and don't even get me started on long division, but I can definitely count."

Martinez shook his head. "No, I mean... Forget it. The point still stands. We're out of our depth here. We need to call in help from the other chapters. There's one in Canada. They could assist."

That Denzel did agree with. If Martinez was going to turn out to be completely useless – and that was looking pretty likely – getting more Spectre Collectors in to help made sense.

"OK, do it," Denzel said.

Martinez fiddled with one of his rings and looked down at his feet. "Can't. The fog is interfering with the signals. Tech and magic – I can't get a message out." He looked up. "I thought we could take a car and drive out of the city. Once we're far enough, we could call for help then."

"You mean run away?" said Denzel.

"No! I mean beat a strategic retreat and consolidate our armies," said Martinez. "It's good strategy. You saw that thing! I mean, I only caught a glimpse but I don't even think it was a shark. I think it was a Megalodon. As in a prehistoric shark. As in the largest predator that ever lived. How are we supposed to fight that?"

Denzel held Martinez's gaze for several seconds. Martinez, eventually, looked away.

"Smithy?" he said.

"Ymmf?" said Smithy through a mouthful of pizza.

"Find us some weapons. We're going back out there."

"Coming right up!" said Smithy. He set off searching for something to fight the shark with, leaving Martinez and Denzel alone. Martinez kept his eyes on the floor, not meeting Denzel's gaze.

"I told Weinberg I thought you were a coward," Denzel said. He saw the look of shame on Martinez's face and immediately felt guilty. "You know what she said? She said you get it together when it counts."

Pointing upwards, Denzel continued. "Now. Now is when it counts."

"I ... I can't," Martinez whispered.

An uncomfortable silence fell, and was eventually broken by Smithy's return. "I could only find these," he said.

Denzel turned to his friend. He stared at him for quite a long time, not quite sure how to react.

Smithy looked like he'd raided a toy shop, with a quick stop off at an office supplies store on the way back. In one hand he held something that looked like a small standing lamp wrapped in wires, while in the other he clutched what might have been an alien death ray, but could equally have been one of those overpriced water guns that can soak a target from thirty metres away.

There were six, seven ... no, *eight* smaller devices tucked into his trousers and socks, or hanging out of his pockets. One of these looked like the ray-gun pistol Denzel had picked up earlier. A few others looked like variations on the first, while at least one, Denzel reckoned, might well have been a banana.

Slung over Smithy's shoulder was something that looked not unlike a bazooka, with lights flashing along the side. A couple of walkie-talkies were clipped on to his belt, and he'd also found a strip of red cloth, which he'd taken the time to tie around his head like a headband.

"I thought you were going to get us weapons?" Denzel said, once he'd finished looking his friend up and down.

"I did. I got these," said Smithy. He waggled the thing that was a bit like a lamp. "This is an Ecto-Thurmoriser. So the box said, anyway."

"What does it do?"

Smithy shrugged. "Thurmorises stuff, probably."

Denzel frowned. "And what does that involve?"

"Dunno," Smithy admitted. He nodded towards the lift. "Let's go and find out."

Drawing in a deep breath, Denzel nodded. "You're right. Let's do it."

They both headed for the lift. Martinez hung back, pacing from foot to foot.

"You need to get above it," he blurted, just as the lift doors opened. Denzel jammed a foot against the door, then turned. Martinez cleared his throat. "The fog. You should find a high point, try to see what's happening. Maybe you can attack the shark from above."

"Like fishing," said Smithy.

"Yeah. Like fishing," said Martinez.

"Come with us," Denzel urged. "If you help, maybe we can still save Weinberg."

Martinez didn't even waste a second considering this. He looked down and turned away.

Without a word, Denzel stepped through into the lift. The doors closed and Smithy barely had time to phase through them before the lift began to climb.

"Any idea how we're going to get back to the van?" Smithy asked.

Denzel took a deep breath. "We're not going back to the van," he said. "Not yet."

The doors opened on the ground floor, revealing a scene of chaos. Men, women and children cowered inside the building's foyer. Harvey was still sitting behind his desk, trying to calm six different people who all screamed at him at the same time in at least three different languages.

A bearded man with wide, hysterical eyes rushed towards the open lift doors. Denzel quickly jabbed the "door close" button. "I'd probably wait for the next one," he said as the doors closed and the lift began to climb.

"Where are we going?" asked Smithy.

"Up," said Denzel, trying to hide the shake in his voice. "We're going all the way up."

As the lift continued its ascent, Denzel thought – not for the first time that day – that he probably should've gone to the toilet.

SPECTRE COLLECTORS

The doors opened on the one-hundred-and-second floor. This was the observation deck, a large viewing area with large fences and windows around the edge to prevent anyone falling off. It was more than high enough to give Denzel and Smithy a view out over the city, but there were forty or more people in there, all staring out. Denzel didn't have any memory dust, so – unfortunate as it was – they had no choice but to sneak into the stairwell, climb the barricade and head for the top floor.

Unlike last time, when the wind had whipped at them, the air was deathly still. Even so, Denzel slid out of the narrow doorway and kept himself pressed flat against the wall.

He had hoped they'd be well above the fog at this height, but no such luck. The fog up here was different though. It was white, like regular, non-supernatural fog. The green stuff stopped abruptly a few metres below them, high enough to cover almost the entire city, aside from the odd skyscraper spire sticking upwards like the masts of old shipwrecks.

Now that he couldn't see how far away the ground was, Denzel found himself feeling less afraid. He risked taking a step away from the wall and was relieved to find he didn't immediately trip over the small surrounding wall and plummet to his death.

"It's like the ocean," said Smithy. And he was right. The green fog was like a vast flood, covering all of New York. In a way, that made sense. The shark – or Megalodon, if Martinez was right – had swum through the mist as if it were swimming through the sea.

"So is this, like, ghost water?" Denzel wondered.

Smithy sniffed the air. "Do you smell that?"

"Yeah, that was me," said Denzel. "Sorry. I don't like heights."

"No, not that. The other smell. It's like back when whatshername opened the Spectral Realm last week." Smithy pointed to the fog. "I think this is Spectrum Density."

It took a few seconds for Denzel to translate. "Spectral Energy?"

"That's the one."

They looked out over the vast ocean of green. "What, all of it?"

"Dunno. Maybe." Smithy shrugged. "Pity the spike isn't working. It could have sucked all this right up."

Denzel nodded. "Yeah, but you heard what Weinberg said. Vulterons have been trying to fix it for..."

The sentence stumbled to a stop as a new thought derailed it. Vulterons had been trying to fix the spike for decades, with no success.

Vulterons.

"Give me a radio, quick," said Denzel. Smithy still had both hands full, so he angled his hip to Denzel and let him grab a walkie-talkie for himself.

"Martinez," said Denzel, thumbing the button. "Martinez, come in, over."

He released the button and waited. It took several seconds, but then the speaker squawked. "Martinez. What do you want, Denzel? I told you, I'm not coming out. Over."

"The spike," Denzel blurted. "Weinberg told us that the Vulterons had tried to fix the spike. What about the Oberons?"

He chewed his lip as he waited for an answer.

"You didn't say 'over'," Smithy pointed out.

"Over."

"It's tech," said Martinez. "That's Vulterons' department. Over."

"But the Spectre Collectors – it's a mix of magic and tech, right? So what if this is the same? What if that's why no one has ever been able to get it working? Over."

There was a long silence. Denzel was about to press the button to speak again when Martinez's voice came crackling out of the earpiece.

"I guess. Maybe."

Another long pause.

"I suppose I could check it out." He groaned. "Fine, I'll head up. Over and out."

Denzel nodded and clipped the radio on to his belt. It was a long shot, but if they could get the spike working, maybe they could clean this mess up. Of course, the ghost of a prehistoric shark was still out there somewhere, and dealing with that was the main priority.

Denzel was about to suggest heading down when a voice whispered at him through the fog. He couldn't be sure which direction it had come from. In fact, if pressed, he'd probably have to say it came from all directions at once.

He is coming.

"He is coming," Denzel said, repeating the words out loud.

Smithy blinked. "Is he?" he asked.

"Apparently," said Denzel.

Smithy shrugged. "Fair enough," he said. He sniffed. "Who is?"

It was Denzel's turn to shrug. "Dunno."

He is coming.

"So you can't hear that?" Denzel asked.

Smithy listened. "Hear what?" he said.

HE IS COMING!

"That?"

Smithy listened again. "Was it a sort of creaking, groany noise, like old wood?"

Denzel started to shake his head, but then stopped. He *could* hear a creaking, groany sort of noise. It came from out in the fog – the white stuff, not the green – somewhere just ahead.

There was a shape out there. It was just a faint outline in the mist right now, but the edges were becoming more defined as the shape grew larger. Whatever it was, it was bigger than the shark, and it was getting closer.

Denzel quietly cleared his throat. "I think, maybe, I should get a gun."

"Take this," said Smithy, handing Denzel the Ecto-Thurmoriser. Denzel took it, and was trying to figure out where the trigger was when Smithy pulled something that looked like an old-fashioned bike horn from his waistband. It was a looping curve of metal with a bulbous black ball on one end that looked designed to be squeezed. "Here, you can have this one," he said, passing it to Denzel and taking the larger weapon back.

Denzel looked longingly at the Ecto-Thurmoriser. "What? I thought I was getting that one?"

"Hmm? Oh, no. Sorry, I just needed you to hold it while I got the other one out. I didn't have enough hands," Smithy explained. He rested the butts of both the Thurmoriser and the big water-blaster-like weapon against his hips and pointed them vaguely in the direction of the shape approaching through the fog. "You'll be fine with that one."

"What am I meant to do with this, *parp* the ghosts to death?" Denzel asked.

"They're already dead," Smithy pointed out.

Denzel tutted. "You know what I mean."

Whatever was out there was almost on them now. With a final *creak*, a deformed, dragon-like head glided free of the mist, its eyes wide, its mouth open, revealing dozens of teeth and a long, curled tongue.

Yelping in shock, Denzel raised the horn-thing, but stopped himself squeezing the end just in time. The dragon's head was not, in fact, a dragon's head. It was a carving of one, done with the same skill and attention to detail as the underwater door had been.

He is coming.

He is coming.

HE IS COMING.

The voices hissed at him from all sides, as if the fog itself was speaking the words.

"He is coming," Denzel repeated.

Something whistled through the air, passed between

Smithy and Denzel, and embedded itself deep into the wall. It was a metal spike, like a harpoon. A length of rope was attached to it, and as Denzel and Smithy watched, a muscle-bound figure with a bristly beard came sliding along the rope towards them.

"Wrong, lad!" boomed a voice. The figure reached the end of the rope and dropped on to the floor beside them. For a moment, Denzel would have sworn the building shook with the impact.

He looked up.

And up.

Eventually, Denzel found the man's face. Between the enormous blond beard and the helmet the man wore, there wasn't a lot of face to see – just a pair of piercingly blue eyes, and a lopsided grin.

"He is not 'coming'. He is *here*!"

CHAPTER 17

As well as not being an expert on geography, Denzel wasn't exactly particularly well versed in history either. Despite that, he would be prepared to bet the man towering over him and Smithy was a Viking.

The bristly blond beard was one clue. The helmet, complete with a metal faceplate and two stubby curved horns sticking out of each side, was another.

The fact there was now a *stupidly big* Viking longship floating in the air just a few metres away had helped make his mind up too. It was around fifteen metres long, with a tall mast and a billowing white sail. It sat almost level with the building's top floor, and although the fog clinging to the deck made it impossible to see, Denzel was sure he could hear movement from the deck. Whoever this guy was, he hadn't come alone.

Smithy leaned past the Viking so he could see Denzel. "Friend of yours?" he asked.

"What? No," said Denzel. He craned his neck again and looked up into the big man's grinning face. He seemed friendly enough. Or friendlier than a prehistoric shark, at least. "Who are you?"

"The name's Ragnarok," the Viking boomed. He took hold of Denzel's hand and shook it in a way that suggested he couldn't just crush every bone in it, but rip the whole thing off at the elbow. Then probably eat it. "You shall call me Rok."

Rok pointed a finger at the top of Denzel's head. "May I?"

"Uh ... may you what?" Denzel asked, but the Viking hadn't waited for an answer. He leaned down until his nose was right above Denzel's head and sniffed deeply.

"He can't help it. He's scared of heights," Smithy explained.

"Aha!" cried Rok, leaning back. He tapped himself on the side of the nose. Quite violently, Denzel thought. "Never fails. You're the one who broke the seal. You opened the doors. Yes?"

Denzel tried to read the Viking's face, trying to determine what the right answer was. Or, rather, what answer was less likely to make the big man angry. With all that beard and helmet, though, it wasn't an easy face to read.

"Uh ... yes?" he said, then all the air was squeezed out of him when Rok picked him up in a bear hug.

"Do you have any idea how long I had been trapped down there? Frozen like the Frost Giants of Jötunheimr? Too long, my young friend. Far too long!"

Rok released his grip, and Denzel had to grab hold of Smithy to stop himself staggering over the edge.

"Well, I suppose ... you're welcome," said Denzel.

"Aye," said Rok, grinning. "I know!"

With a tug, he pulled the harpoon out of the wall. "And now I'm free. I'm back. And that monster of the deep won't know what hit it!"

Denzel and Smithy exchanged a glance. "Wait," said Denzel. "Monster of the deep? You know about that thing?"

"Ha! The beast has been my mortal enemy for centuries. I was on the brink of besting it when we were banished. Thanks to you, the chase can finally continue."

Denzel and Smithy both watched in amazement as Rok bent the end of the metal harpoon into a hook shape.

"Cor, he's strong, innhe?" said Smithy. He reached up and prodded one of the muscles bulging beneath the Viking's leather jerkin. "That's like a baby's head, that is."

"So you're going to catch it?" asked Denzel. This was perfect! If Rok dealt with the Megalodon, Denzel and Smithy might not even have to get involved.

"Aye! I just need you to assist me in one final matter."

Denzel and Smithy exchanged a glance, then both shrugged. "OK," said Denzel. "What do you want me to do?"

In one swift move, Rok snagged Denzel's belt on his metal hook, then stepped up on to the ledge. "I want you to be bait!" he said, then, with a single bounding leap, he threw himself on to the deck of his ship.

It all happened so quickly, Denzel barely had time to react. He had just started to turn to see what Rok had done to his belt when the big Viking tugged on the rope. Denzel's eyes went wide as he was dragged backwards.

"Smithy!" he yelped. The back of his legs hit the railing. The world lurched. The last thing he saw was Smithy tossing aside the Ecto-Thurmoriser and big water-blaster weapon, and diving towards him. And then Denzel was falling, plunging, plummeting down, down, down through the swirling green fog.

He tried to scream but was far too terrified to actually

make any sound beyond a sort of high-pitched wheeze. The hook jerked him as the rope went tight, knocking the wind out of him so he couldn't even manage the wheeze any more.

With the rope tight, Denzel swung in a swooping arc, spinning around and around as he *swooshed* through the fog.

"Wheeeeeee!"

Denzel looked down. For the first time, he realised Smithy was holding on to both his wrists.

"All right?" said Smithy, in what Denzel couldn't help but feel was far too calm a manner, what with the circumstances.

"Not really," he managed to gasp in return. "Had b-better days."

Something screamed at them through the fog. A white shape, like a flapping sheet, hurtled towards them, eyes and mouth wide open. The rope twisted, spinning them out of the shape's path just in time.

"What was that?" Denzel hissed.

"A ghost, I think," said Smithy.

"It's coming back!"

Smithy reached for a banana-shaped weapon tucked in his belt, leaving Denzel frantically trying to hold on to him by one arm. As the ghost wailed towards them,

Smithy opened fire with the banana gun. A little red blob emerged from the end and tumbled slowly through the air.

As the ghost met the blob, there was a blinding red flash and a surge of energy that sent the rope swinging violently in a wide swooshing curve. The glass front of a building loomed out of the fog. As they swung towards it, Denzel could see dozens of people pressed up against the windows, watching in disbelief. A little girl, around six years old, waved at them as they went spinning by. Smithy smiled and waved back, then he turned and blasted another ghost that came screeching out of the green haze.

"Where are they coming from?" Denzel wailed, as the force of the exploding spook sent them into another out-of-control spin.

He could probably guess the answer. They had to have come from the same place as Rok and the shark had – the undersea doors. That meant them being here was Denzel's fault. He just wished they were as grateful as Rok had been. Although, as Rok's gratitude had led to Denzel swinging from a rope a hundred storeys above the ground, perhaps that might actually be for the best.

The boat was moving now, dragging Denzel and Smithy along behind it. Denzel's muscles strained with the effort of holding on to Smithy and his belt was cutting painfully into his waist.

When he spun just the right way, Denzel was able to see the underside of the longship. Several sets of oars were moving in harmony, propelling the boat across the surface of the fog ocean.

Another shape came fluttering out of the mist. Smithy opened fire but the ghost banked away and was quickly lost to the mist. Denzel held his breath for a few seconds, waiting to see if it came back, but there was no sign of it.

Smithy smiled up at him. "You know, I've never been fishing before," he said. "It's quite exciting."

Denzel had never been fishing before either, but he was pretty sure it wasn't usually like this. Not unless you were the worm, anyway.

He was about to say as much when he saw the shape looming in the fog beneath them. It had to be ten storeys lower than they were, and most of the detail was hidden by the mist. It had looked big when it was chasing them, but from this angle it somehow managed to appear even larger.

Denzel held his breath. He could almost hear the *Jaws* theme playing in his head. And then he realised that he could hear it in his ears too. Smithy was humming it.

"Cut it out!" Denzel whispered.

"Sorry," said Smithy. "Just seemed appropriate."

The Megalodon flicked its tail, twitched its fins, and then, to Denzel's horror – although, to be honest, he was kind of expecting it, what with the way his day had been going so far – it began to swim upwards.

CHAPTER 18

"What would you rather, right? Only be able to eat crisps, or *never*—"

"Seriously? You're doing this *now*?"

"What? Oh, yeah. Fair point," said Smithy. He looked down. "Shark's coming."

"I know!"

"Quite quickly too."

"Yes, thank you, Smithy, I noticed!" said Denzel.

Smithy looked at the banana-shaped ray gun in his hand. He looked down at the shark, which now appeared bigger than ever as it sliced upwards through the fog.

"I don't think that thing's going to do much good,"

Denzel warned him.

"Don't be so sure, Denzel. Size isn't everything!" said Smithy.

He shot at the shark. The red blob fell, *pinged* off the monster's hide, then tumbled off into the fog.

"No, you're right, that was rubbish," Smith admitted.

"Ragnarok!" Denzel shouted. "It's here. Pull us up!"

Nothing happened. Well, nothing that didn't involve Denzel and Smithy continuing to dangle from a rope above the ghost of a prehistoric shark, at least.

"I'm not convinced he heard you," said Smithy. He let go of Denzel's hands and floated in the air beside him. "Want me to pop up?"

Denzel gaped at his friend in surprise, then down at his own hands. "Wait, why was I holding you up? You can fly!"

"I'll go tell thingummyjig to pull you up," said Smithy.

"*You* pull me up!" Denzel yelped. "Fly me out of here."

Smithy shook his head. "Not strong enough on my own. I could probably slow you down if you fell, but that's it. Be right back!"

"Wait!" Denzel cried. He pointed to the weapon slung over Smithy's shoulder. "Give me the bazooka!"

"It's not a bazooka, it's a Boomzooka," said Smithy. "Look, it's written on the side."

"I don't care!" yelped Denzel. "Just give me it!"

Smithy glanced back at it. "I don't know. It's probably pretty dangerous."

"*Hello!* Giant shark!" Denzel cried.

Smithy looked down. The shark was close enough to pick out details now. A fin. A dark eye. Many, *many* teeth.

"Fair point, well made," Smithy admitted. He unhooked the bazooka and handed it to Denzel. "OK, back soon. Don't go anywhere."

"I'll try my best," Denzel said. "But hurry!"

Smithy shot upwards and was quickly lost in the fog. Denzel studied the weapon, his hands shaking. He was almost grateful for the fog. Without it, he'd have been able to see the ground, and if he could see the ground he'd probably be frozen with fear.

Instead, he was able to get his shaking under control long enough to spin the end of the launcher weapon towards the approaching shark, then squeeze off a shot.

KAWOOOSH!

Some sort of energy missile exploded from the bazooka's muzzle. Unfortunately, Denzel had pointed it the wrong way, and it streaked backwards away from the approaching shark, while at the same time launching him forwards on the rope as if he was on a tyre swing.

Somewhere in the distance, something exploded.

Denzel hoped it was nothing important.

He swung back down just as the shark charged. Its scarred snout emerged from the fog first, followed by one cold, dead eye. It snapped hungrily, but Denzel's swing took him out of its path, and the monster had to turn its whole body before it could come in for another attack.

"Hurry up!" Denzel shouted upwards, as he wrestled the bazooka around the right way. The Megalodon had already pulled off a full turn, and was racing back towards him again, its powerful tail hurtling it through the fog.

Denzel braced himself and pulled the trigger. This time, he had pointed it in the right direction. He was sent hurtling backwards by the momentum as the missile spat from the bazooka and exploded against the shark's head.

The monster thrashed and spasmed violently. It had felt that one. To Denzel's dismay, though, it didn't explode, implode, turn into vapour or any of the other things he'd been hoping the weapon might do to it. Instead, it just slowed down for a while, spent a few seconds drifting aimlessly, then jerked back into life.

As he swung, Denzel looked down at the weapon. There had been three little red lights illuminated on the barrel when Smithy had given it to him. Now there was one. One shot left. One last chance to stop this thing before it swallowed him whole.

Or worse – swallowed him *not* whole.

The hook jerked suddenly. At first, Denzel thought his belt had snapped, and let out what he felt was an entirely appropriate amount of screaming.

When he didn't start plunging towards the ground, though, he realised what had really happened. The rope was being pulled up. Rok was reeling him in!

But not quickly enough. The Megalodon, sensing it might be about to lose its prey, swam faster, its head snapping left and right as it used all its strength to close the gap. Denzel fumbled with the bazooka, but before he could fire, a shape streaked up from below and slammed into the shark's underside.

No, not a shape. A person.

"Weinberg!" Denzel cried.

Weinberg had the drone-like device Denzel had seen in the weapons crate strapped to her back, and one of the gauntlets on each hand. She pressed both palms against the Megalodon's hide and something like an electrical charge rippled through it. The great beast turned its head and snapped at her, but a blue light flared on the backpack and Weinberg zipped down, out of its reach.

"Denzel, the mouth!" Weinberg cried. She caught hold

of the Megalodon's bottom lip, pulsed another couple of glove-blasts into it, then yanked down as hard as she could.

Denzel froze as, for a moment, all he could see was the shark's teeth, blood-red mouth and gaping, cave-like insides.

And then, with a twitch of his finger, he fired the last remaining shot down the shark's throat. As before, the momentum launched him up and backwards. Weinberg released her grip and turned, just as the Megalodon erupted in an explosion of ectoplasmic goo.

"Yes!" Denzel cried, but his joy didn't last long. The unexpected ectoplasm shower had done something to Weinberg's drone pack. She juddered up and down in the air as the backpack's power fluctuated wildly.

"Uh-oh!" she hissed, then she diverted all the pack's power into climbing. Tearing off the gloves, she tossed them aside and made a grab for the end of the bazooka, which Denzel was holding out to her.

Her fingers brushed against the metal, but then the backpack shuddered again and she lost altitude.

"Bit higher!" Denzel shouted. It wasn't particularly helpful, he knew, but it was the best he could come up with.

The drone stuttered, the blue light flickering, but then

a sudden boost of power lifted Weinberg high enough to grab the bazooka. She clutched it with both hands and Denzel's belt creaked in protest at the extra weight. His arms didn't exactly thank him either, but he gritted his teeth and managed to hold on until they bumped against the side of the longship and two powerful hands heaved them aboard.

They landed heavily on the deck and Denzel quickly unhooked the bent harpoon from his trousers.

"Who is this?" demanded Rok, towering over them. Smithy stood beside him, grinning proudly.

"It's fine, she's with us," he said. "We thought she was dead, but ... wait, you're not dead, are you?"

"No, Smithy," said Weinberg. "Close, but not quite."

"Bah! I care not," boomed Ragnarok. He shoved the Spectre Collectors aside and leaned out over the edge of the boat.

Denzel stood up, then almost shrieked in fright when he saw who was working the ship's oars. The boat had, in every sense, a skeleton crew. Eight skeletons, their bones yellowed and browning with age, sat on low benches, heaving the oars in perfect time. They all grinned at Denzel when he spotted them. At least, he thought they grinned at him, but maybe all jawbones looked like that.

"Where is it? Where is the beast?" Rok demanded.

"We blew it up," said Denzel. "We got it!"

"All *right*," said Smithy. He jumped up and gave Denzel a high-five. Rok, on the other hand, looked less impressed.

"Excuse me?" he said, turning slowly. "What did you say?"

"We blew it up," said Denzel.

Half buried in his beard, Rok's mouth twisted into a sneer.

"I hope, for your sake, that I misunderstand what you are telling me," the Viking growled. "So, just so we're clear, tell me again."

Denzel shot Smithy and Weinberg a couple of nervous glances. "Well, I mean, it was coming after me, it was going to get me, and so..." He swallowed. "I blew it up. I blew up the shark."

Rok's snarl deepened for a moment, then he erupted in a loud, roaring sort of laugh. "Oh, you almost had me worried for a moment," he said, grabbing Denzel by the back of the neck and shaking him violently. It was supposed to be a friendly gesture, Denzel guessed, but it almost took his head off. "Shark?" Rok laughed. "Who said anything about a shark? It's not a shark I'm after. It's the beast."

Denzel frowned. He looked across to Weinberg, but

she just shrugged. Smithy was staring past him, his eyes wide, paying Denzel no attention.

"So if it wasn't the shark, then what's the beast?" Denzel asked.

Slowly, his arm shaking, Smithy pointed off through the fog. A squid-like tentacle, easily eight storeys high, curled up from beneath the surface of the fog.

"I could be wrong, but I'm guessing *that's* probably it, over there."

CHAPTER 19

"Hard astern!" roared Rok, in a voice that almost made Denzel's eardrums explode.

The skeletons began to row in different directions, as two others adjusted the ship's sail. The ship slowly began to turn, the carved dragon head angling around towards the towering tentacle.

"What is that thing?" Denzel asked. He wanted to ask more, but his whole body had gone rigid with fear, and just getting those four words out had been hard enough.

Rok laughed and slapped Denzel on the back. It was like being pranged by a small family car. "That, lad, is the great beast itself. Behold, the mighty Kraken!"

The Viking turned and shouted back over his shoulder. "Harpoons at the ready! There'll be no getting away from us this time!"

The skeletons all jumped up from their benches. The oars continued to row all by themselves. Normally, Denzel would have considered this to be pretty amazing, but what with everything else going on, he barely even noticed.

"What are you going to do?" demanded Weinberg. Even though Rok was practically double her height, she had her hands on her hips and was fixing him with a look that bordered on being aggressive.

"Nothing for a female to worry her pretty little head about," said Rok, without so much as glancing Weinberg's way.

Denzel winced. From the way Weinberg's expression darkened, that remark hadn't gone down well.

"Answer the question," she said. "What are you going to do?"

With a distracted sigh, Rok half turned and shoved Weinberg back. She reacted quickly, hooking one arm around his wrist, bending back his thumb, then swinging her whole body up so one foot was pressed against the big Viking's throat.

"I am a Vulteron in the Seventh Army of the

Enlightened," she told him. "You are an unauthorised Spectral Entity within the boundaries of *my* jurisdiction. You *will* answer the question."

Smithy leaned closer to Denzel. "That's the most awesome thing I've ever seen," he whispered.

Rok snorted in amusement, raised his arm, then flicked. Weinberg sailed several metres through the air and slammed into the ship's mast, before flopping on to the deck.

"Oh, no, I take it back," said Smithy. "*That* was."

"Stay out of my way, child!" Rok warned her. Around him, the skeletons were racing across the deck, all carrying spears with ropes attached. Their bony feet *tick-ticked* on the wooden floor as they scurried to the bow of the ship. Or, as Denzel thought of it, "the front bit".

Weinberg flipped back to her feet and began charging along the deck. Denzel caught her before she could try another attack.

"Whoa, whoa, wait!" he said. "Stop. What are you doing?"

"He's an unauthorised Spectral Entity," Weinberg said. "I'm taking him down."

"Well, I mean, yeah, that's one way of looking at it," said Denzel. "Another way of looking at it is that he's about to stop a giant—"

"Huge," added Smithy.

"—ghost octopus from, well, whatever it is giant ghost octopuses do."

"Pie," said Smithy.

Denzel frowned. "What?"

"It's octopi. Not octopuses."

"It's not," said Denzel. "People think it is, but it isn't. We did it in school."

Smithy pulled a surprised face. "Really? Well, there you go. You learn something new every—"

"Guys!" snapped Weinberg. She gestured to where Rok was now standing right up on the bow, one arm hooked over the dragon's head. Behind him, his skeletal crew stood behind the carved railing, spears raised. Each spear was attached to a length of chain, and each chain was fastened to a heavy metal plate affixed to the deck.

"Oh, yeah, sorry," said Denzel. "My point is, do you really want to have to take down a giant octopus? Or is it better to leave him to it?"

Weinberg ground her teeth together, chewing the idea over. "I mean ... I guess I could wait," she said. "But the second he's done, we're sending him back to where he came from."

She yanked the last of the smaller weapons from Smithy's belt, turned a dial, flipped a lever, then unfolded the whole thing until it was five times the size. "We call this the Thingamajig. It can be adapted to suit most battle situations."

Smithy stared longingly at the weapon, then looked down at the tiny ray gun he was still holding. "Can mine do that?" he asked.

"Depends. Do you want it to work afterwards?" Weinberg asked.

"Well, ideally, yeah," Smithy replied.

Weinberg shrugged. "Then no. Sorry."

Denzel turned the bazooka over in his hands. All three lights were now dim. He pulled the trigger to check if it was empty. Luckily for all concerned, it was.

"Can you reload this?" he asked, holding it up.

Weinberg shook her head. "Not here."

"Great. So what do I do?"

"You could hit people with it," Smithy suggested. "Not us. Bad people, I mean. Or bad octopi."

"Octopuses," said Denzel. He held the bazooka like a club and gave it an experimental swish. It was better than having no weapon at all, but only just.

"First wave, go!" Ragnarok's voice rumbled the deck beneath their feet. Up front, four skeletons hurled their spears into the fog.

Even before the first lot had found their target, the

second wave was stepping up, spears held above their bare skulls like javelins.

Three of the first waves hit the exposed tentacle with a series of slightly squelchy *thunks*. Ragnarok clenched a fist in triumph, then pointed to the left, where a second tentacle was rising out of the mist, uncurling as it reached for the ship. The suckers on the tentacle's underside were the size of tractor tyres, and Denzel couldn't shake the feeling that harpooning this thing was only going to get on its nerves.

"Wave two, unleash Hell!"

Chains rattled across the decks as the spears flew. All four found the target this time. The tentacle snapped back as the hooks sunk into its flesh.

"We've hooked it!" Ragnarok boomed. "By Odin, after all these centuries, we've finally hooked it!"

"Great," said Weinberg. "Well done. Now what?"

The chains jerked tight as the monster sunk back down beneath the fog. With a clank of metal, a groan of wood and a scream of Denzel, the longship dipped sharply at the front, until the back end was angled upwards into the air.

Denzel and Weinberg skidded down the now sloping deck, kicking and scrabbling at the wood. Smithy, who was less affected by gravity, hung back for a minute before clearly deciding it looked like fun, and throwing himself after them.

"Oof!" Denzel hit the front railing of the boat, just before Weinberg crunched into him.

A moment later, Smithy slammed into them both, shouting, "Wheee!"

Thanks to the whole "ghosts v gravity" thing, Rok and the skeletons were all standing on the tilting deck with no difficulty whatsoever.

"It's going to pull us down!" Denzel cried.

"Aye, maybe," Rok admitted. He held out a hand and the air around it shimmered. A large, double-headed battle-axe materialised in his grip. His fingers tightened around the twine-wrapped handle. "But maybe not!"

With a wink, the big Viking ran towards the bow. His long blond beard flapped in the wind as he threw himself over the edge. Raising the axe above his head, Ragnarok shouted something as he plunged into the fog. It was in a language Denzel didn't understand, but he was pretty confident it involved quite a lot of swearing.

And then he was gone, and there was no sound from the ship except the clanking of the chains and the creaking of the wood.

Smithy stood up and peered down into the fog. There was a sort of delirious expression on his face. "I *so* want to be like him when I grow up!"

A skeletal hand caught him by the back of his neck. Smithy frowned as the ghost's bony fingers squeezed. "Hey. You've grabbed my neck," he said, in case the skeleton somehow hadn't noticed. It clamped another hand on his throat and began to squeeze, trying to choke the life out of him.

Smithy shot Denzel a slightly awkward look. "I think he's trying to strangle me. Bit embarrassing." He addressed the skeleton again. "You do know I'm a ghost too? This is going to get you nowhere."

Denzel gulped as three of the other skeletons turned to glare at him, their toothy grins seeming to creep higher up their cheeks as they fixed him with their hollow stares.

"Uh, is it just me, or do you get the impression these guys don't like us?"

"The Viking was their leader," Weinberg said. "Without him, they're resorting to their natural state."

"Which is?"

"Pretty unpleasant."

One of the skeletons giving Denzel the evil eye began creeping towards him.

"Back off," Weinberg warned. The skeleton skulked closer, its fingers curving into claws. "I am a Vulteron in the Seventh Army of the Enlightened," said Weinberg. "You are an unauthorised Spectral— Oh, forget it."

She squeezed the trigger of the Thingamajig and a thin beam of energy streaked from the barrel. The skeleton exploded like an overfilled water bomb, splattering the deck in a fine mist of ectoplasm.

That did it. The six remaining skeletons – not counting the one still trying in vain to choke Smithy – divided themselves up, three each, between Denzel and Weinberg. Then, with a rattle of ancient bones and a roar of supernatural rage, they attacked.

CHAPTER 20

Weinberg fired off another shot that splattered a skeleton into lumpy jelly, but she couldn't turn in time to take aim again. Bony fingers grabbed for her weapon, as sharp, angular knees and elbows pinned her against the deck.

Denzel, to his own immense surprise, was actually faring better. He swung out with the Boomzooka at knee-height, and one of the skeletons lost both legs from the thigh bone down.

Another lunged at him, but Denzel thrust the end of the bazooka up at it. Metal met skull with a deeply satisfying *ker-ack*.

Denzel tried to stand, but the boat was tilting even further now. As he looked up at the stern – or, as he knew it, "the back bit" – Denzel was hit by a strong feeling of déjà vu. This all seemed terribly familiar somehow, like he'd lived through it before.

Had he been thinking more rationally, he would have realised he was simply remembering the final half-hour of the film *Titanic*, but right now, logical thought was the last thing on his mind.

Weinberg flicked up a leg, driving a powerful kick into the side of a skeleton's head. The skull snapped off, bounced across the deck, then rolled over the edge and into the mist below.

"You're just not taking the hint, are you?" Smithy said to the skeleton, who was, despite everything, still trying to choke him. Its grin was still fixed on its face, but there was frustration in the hollows of its eyes now.

Rather than change its tactics, though, it had doubled down and was trying to squeeze harder. Smithy's head grew a little larger, like an inflating balloon, but otherwise he suffered no real ill effects.

Denzel's Boomzooka landed a glancing blow on another skeleton's hip. It wobbled slightly, but then found its balance and dived on him, its teeth gnashing hungrily, its fingers creeping through his hair.

"Get off!" he hissed, pushing back against the thing. It was too strong though; its grip too powerful. Despite being nothing but bones – and ghost bones, at that – it was too heavy for him to be able to throw it off.

Weinberg was wrestling with the last of the three skeletons that had attacked her too. She jammed both thumbs into its eye sockets but it had no effect. Instead, she caught hold of its bottom jaw, placed her other hand flat on its forehead and heaved.

The jawbone snapped. The skeleton tried to pull back but Weinberg grabbed its skull and twisted until it popped loose. With a grunt of effort, she lobbed the skull backwards over her head, where it was quickly lost to the swirling fog.

Denzel punched the other skeleton right where its nose would have been, if it still had one. Pain ignited in his knuckles as they smashed against the hard skull, and Denzel spent the next few seconds muttering, "Ow, ow, ow!" while trying, very hard, not to die.

The skeleton's hands moved to Denzel's throat. Unlike Smithy, Denzel relied quite heavily on his windpipe, so when the creature's weight pressed down on it, he kicked and struggled and—

KASPLOOSH.

The skeleton dissolved in a gush of ecto-gloop. The

goo hung in the air in a vague skeleton shape for a half-second or so, then fell in a downpour on Denzel, just as he opened his mouth to gasp for air.

"Ugh! Ew! I've got ghost in my mouth!" he spluttered.

Weinberg stood supporting herself on the starboard rail, a glowing blue smoke curling from the barrel of the Thingamajig.

"You're welcome," she said, then she turned and, with a single blast, obliterated the final skeleton.

"Thanks for that," said Smithy. "I thought he was never going to stop."

He turned, just as Denzel looked up.

"Oh, my *God!*" Denzel spluttered. "Smithy! Your head!"

"What about it?" asked Smithy. He reached a hand up and found his cheek. It would have been difficult to miss. His head had swollen to four times its normal size. It teetered unsteadily atop a neck that was roughly as thick as a broom handle. "Ooh, boy. Yeah. That's large. That *is* large."

He placed both hands over his ears and squeezed. His forehead and nose both bulged outwards.

"No, that's made it worse, if anything," he muttered.

The radio on Denzel's belt squawked. "Denzel?" said Martinez. "What's going on? Over."

Denzel unhooked the radio and thumbed the button. "Long story. There's a Viking and a big octopus. Did you fix the spike?"

He released the button and waited.

"You need to say 'over'," Weinberg reminded him, but before Denzel could say anything, three of the groaning chains snapped and the longship jerked backwards. Denzel and Weinberg were tossed into the air.

When they hit the deck again, the walkie-talkie was knocked from Denzel's grasp. It slid away from him down the deck, picking up speed as it hurtled towards the edge.

"I got it, I got it!" said Smithy. He staggered towards the radio, only for his enormous head to throw him off balance. He bent, trying to grab for the walkie-talkie, but his forehead hit the railing with a hollow *clonk* and the device slid off the deck and down into the fog below. "No, wait, I tell a lie."

The four remaining chains didn't break, but they went suddenly slack, as if the octopus, or Kraken, or whatever it was, had managed to pull itself free.

The longship rocked violently but then settled on to an even keel. Denzel quickly got to his feet and scooped the worst of the ecto-slime off his face. He could still taste it at the back of his throat. It reminded him of stagnant water and old socks. With, weirdly enough, a not-unpleasant pepperminty aftertaste.

Weinberg was already up front, leaning on the railing, her rifle sweeping the fog below. Smithy stood beside her, repeatedly slapping himself in the face as he tried to batter his head back into shape. It was now the size of a watermelon, but with the shape and texture of a cabbage. Still, it was a step in the right direction.

"See anything?" Denzel asked.

Weinberg shook her head. "No visuals, and no scanners on this thing," she said. "If I had to guess, I'd say your Viking friend probably didn't make it. Which leaves us with a problem."

One of the dangling chains rattled, then swung violently across the deck, forcing Denzel and Weinberg to jump. Smithy didn't bother, and the chain passed harmlessly through his ankles before snagging on a railing.

The boat shuddered as the chain went tight again. Denzel grabbed for the mast, trying to get a hold of something before the boat tipped, but there was less pull on the chain this time and the ship remained level.

Either what was attached to the chain wasn't as heavy as before … or it was moving upwards.

Denzel felt his stomach do a little flip as the tip of an

enormous octopus limb appeared out of the fog. It rose a metre or two into the air, twisted limply, then flopped down on to the deck.

Where it had previously been attached to the rest of the tentacle, it was now just a relatively small piece with a ragged edge where it had been sliced off.

The chain rattled again, and a bruised and battered Ragnarok heaved himself on to the deck. His leather jerkin was badly torn and a patch of his blond beard was now missing. One of the horns on his helmet had been snapped off, and there was a slick of ectoplasmic slime across his bare chest.

He no longer had his axe, but his grin was still there, wider than ever. "And *that*, my friends, is how you kill a Kraken!"

"No, it isn't," said Smithy.

Rok looked across the deck. He stopped when he spotted the scattered bones.

"Where is my crew?" he demanded. His eyes narrowed behind the slits of his helmet's visor. Denzel was relieved Rok no longer appeared to have his axe, although there was always the possibility he'd just pull it out of thin air again. "What did you do to them?"

"Hello!" called Smithy. "Yoohoo. Anyone listening?"

"Odin's beard! What happened to his head?" Rok

gasped.

Smithy hammered his forehead a few times, trying to beat it back into shape. One of his ears doubled in size.

"Doesn't matter," he said. He pointed to the tip of the tentacle, twitching on the deck. "I was just saying, that's not how you kill a Kraken."

"Pah! Your words are nonsense, large-headed boy!" Rok snorted. "How would you possibly know that?"

"Well, mainly," said Smithy, "because it's not dead."

Rok, Denzel and Weinberg all turned just as another tentacle finished rising into view behind the ship. The Viking's jaw dropped. He reached out a hand, but this time no axe appeared in it.

"Och," he muttered. "That is most disappointing."

"Stand aside," Weinberg said. She twisted a dial on the side of the Thingamajig, then opened fire. The beam that emerged was a pure, blinding white. Even though he was more than a metre behind Weinberg, the glow from the gun jabbed right at the back of Denzel's eyeballs. He forced himself to keep watching though, as the beam struck the octopus, right on one of its suction cups.

The limb thrashed. The Kraken screeched. And then, with a *pop* that rattled the windows of the buildings below, the beast disintegrated into vapour.

Weinberg turned back to Ragnarok and rested the

Thingamajig on her hip. "Now, *that*," she said, "is how you kill a Kraken."

Rok's jaw dropped. "You destroyed it. You destroyed the great beast!"

"Well, technically I didn't destroy it. It's Spectral Energy; energy can't be destroyed, just transformed. But it'll take it a few hundred years to pull its atoms back together, by which point it'll be contained." Weinberg adjusted the controls of the Thingamajig. "And so will you, blondie."

Before she had a chance to take aim at him, Rok caught the Thingamajig and yanked it from Weinberg's hand. "Fascinating," he said, turning the device over and over. "'Tis a weapon of the gods themselves."

Weinberg dived at Rok, but the Viking turned and dodged without looking up, then tripped her as she passed. She slid across the deck and stopped next to Smithy and Denzel. They both helped her up, then held her back before she could launch herself at the Viking again. He had the Thingamajig trained on her, the weapon looking cartoonishly small in his shovel-like hands.

"I always wondered what I would do once the Kraken was bested. I have hunted that monster in life and death. It was my purpose. My mission. My reason to be." Rok took a step towards them. "And now it is done, and I am adrift. For the first time in a long, long time, I am purposeless."

He took another step closer. "So now I need a new purpose. A new mission. And I have decided what that mission will be."

"That was quick," said Denzel, nervously eyeing the Thingamajig. "It might be best not to rush into anything."

"I am going to do what we Vikings were born to do."

"Start a small farming community?" Smithy guessed. "Brilliant idea. High-five."

Smithy held his hand up but Ragnarok ignored him and took one final step closer to Weinberg. His eyes blazed beneath his helmet's visor. "Conquer." He gestured around him at the handful of buildings that rose above the fog. "Your village – this 'New York' of yours – now belongs to me."

Weinberg shook her head. "Not going to happen," she warned. "Like I said, New York is my jurisdiction and I do not take kindly to Spectral invasions. You are going down."

"Ha!" Ragnarok boomed. "Such spirit! And also, such an appropriate turn of phrase. *Going down*."

His foot raised, then hit Weinberg in the chest like a battering ram. She flew backwards, slamming into Denzel as he scrambled to catch her. They both hit the railing together. The hazy sky overhead was suddenly, briefly, below them, then gravity had them in its clutches and they both fell, screaming, into the fog.

CHAPTER 21

Denzel plunged through the fog, flapping his arms as he tried desperately – and, ultimately, unsuccessfully – to fly. It was not the first time he'd fallen from such a ridiculous height in the last half-hour, but at least last time he'd been attached to a rope. This time he was attached to nothing at all, which meant he would soon be attached to the ground in such a way that he could only be removed with a shovel and a high-pressure hose.

"Hold on, Denzel!"

Smithy's voice came in short bursts through the sound of the wind whistling past. Denzel opened his eyes – which he hadn't actually realised he'd closed – to see his friend hurtling towards him from above.

Weinberg was directly below him, facing the ground, just out of reach. She had screamed for the first second or so, but was now silent. Either she was trying to come up with a clever escape plan, or had resigned herself to the upcoming *splat.*

Smithy dropped past Denzel and matched speed with Weinberg. "Got you!" he said, grabbing for their arms. Once he had them, he gritted his teeth and flew upwards.

Or, rather, he tried to. The rate of descent fell, but not by much, and not enough to prevent the upcoming impact. They were still going to hit the ground. They were still going to die. At best, there'd be less mess to clean up, but otherwise Smithy's rescue plan wasn't proving very effective.

"Smithy!" Denzel cried. He met Smithy's gaze and knew, in that moment, that there was nothing his friend could do. There was nothing anyone could do. They were falling, and they weren't going to stop until they hit the ground.

They stopped, just before they hit the ground. It was quite a sudden stop, but much less sudden than it could have been.

Weinberg and Denzel looked at each other hanging in

the air. Smithy was still holding on to them, but it was clear he wasn't the one holding them up. He released his grip and they all just continued floating there, several metres above a row of abandoned cars.

"Smithy, did you do this?" Denzel asked.

Smithy shook his head. "No. I mean, I don't think so. I mean, not that I noticed. Why, did you?"

"Probably not," said Denzel.

Weinberg looked over her shoulder to check the drone pack, but it was completely dead. Besides, even if it had been working, that wouldn't have explained how Denzel had stopped and was now suspended by nothing but empty space.

"Don't get me wrong, this is definitely better than I was expecting the next three seconds to go," said Denzel. He ran in the air, but didn't go anywhere. "But how do we get down?"

"Well now," called a voice from somewhere just above them in the fog. The outline of someone with a fluttering cape grew larger through the green haze. "Perhaps I can help with that."

"Superman!" cried Smithy. "Hooray, we're saved!"

"Uh, no," said Martinez, emerging from the fog. Flickering lights surrounded his feet and danced around his fingertips. "Just me. Sorry to disappoint."

Weinberg smiled. "Not a disappointment at all, partner."

"Good to see you in one piece, Weinberg," said Martinez. He glanced away. "Sorry I didn't come sooner."

"You're here now," said Denzel. "And that's what counts."

"Yeah," agreed Smithy. "We won't even talk about what a coward you were earlier."

Martinez nodded. "Thanks."

"You know, refusing to come outside and everything."

"Right."

"And wanting to run away."

"Yes, thank you, Smithy. That's very kind of you not to mention any of that stuff," Martinez said, doing his best to smile. "I really appreciate that."

With a wave of his hand, he gently lowered Denzel and Weinberg to the ground. The fog was even thicker down at street level. They could just make out the shapes of a couple of yellow cabs through the green haze, and the only sounds were the echo of their own voices bouncing back at them.

"So what's the situation?" asked Weinberg.

"You mean besides 'Wah, there are ghosts everywhere'?" said Martinez. He gestured into the fog. "This stuff seems to have awoken the city's dormant supernatural entities. We thought they were gone, but I think they've just been ... sleeping, somehow. Without any Spectral Energy to power them up they've been in hibernation mode, but now this stuff has taken them out of it and they're wide awake."

"Like Sea-Monkeys," said Smithy. When everyone frowned at him at the same time, he continued. "You know, those little prehistoric egg things that are all dried up, but when you pour water on them, boom. Sea-Monkeys."

He crossed his arms and took on an expression of annoyance. "Although, I should say, they don't actually turn into monkeys at any point. Personally, I think that should be made *much* clearer on the box."

"Uh, yeah," said Martinez. "Like Sea-Monkeys, I guess."

A flailing white shape emerged from the fog right beside Denzel. Martinez muttered something and waved a finger. The ghost was immediately encased in a film of ice and fell to the ground with a *thunk*.

"Nicely done," said Weinberg.

Martinez bit his lip and smiled. From the way his fingers had trembled, it was obvious he was still terrified. Like Weinberg had said, though, he'd stepped up when it counted.

"What about the spike?" Denzel asked. "Any luck?"

"I told you, that thing's been broken for decades," said Weinberg.

Martinez raised his eyebrows and rocked back on his heels. His smile widened in a way that made him look quite smug.

"You didn't!" said Weinberg.

"Just needed an Oberon touch," Martinez said. "You were right, Denzel."

"Great!" cheered Denzel. "Then we can just switch it on, it'll suck him up and job done. We can all go back to eating pizza and playing Battleface."

"Battle*fist*," said Martinez, Smithy and Weinberg at the same time.

"That too," said Denzel. He grinned hopefully. "That's right, isn't it? That's all we need to do?"

Martinez and Weinberg both shook their heads. "Not that simple," said Martinez. "Sure, it'll eventually drain the Spectral Energy but that's going to take days. Weeks, probably."

"And it doesn't solve the problem of our friend up there," said Weinberg, pointing upwards into the fog. "He's strong. We'd need to get him actually touching the spike for it to work. Reckon we can convince him to do that?"

"No," said Denzel. An idea came at him, like a ghost

out of the mist. It was a silly idea. No, it was an *insane* idea. The others would almost certainly never go along with it. He tried to push it away but it kept coming back. A bit like a Sea-Monkey. Emphasis on that last part.

Denzel smiled. "But I think I might know someone who can."

CHAPTER 22

Weinberg flew in front, the blue glow of her drone-pack leading the way through the pale white mist that hung like a cloud above the ocean of fog. Denzel and Martinez floated behind in a big magic bubble. That wasn't the technical name for it, of course – Martinez had called it the Sacred Sphere of something-or-other – but it was a pretty fitting description, all the same.

Smithy trailed along behind, flying under his own steam. Denzel waved to him through the bubble's transparent walls, and Smithy grinned as he waved back.

It had barely been a week since Denzel had discovered his best friend was a ghost, and he was surprised how quickly he'd got used to the idea. The fact he was flying seemed like the most normal thing in the world.

Then again, Smithy had never been even close to normal.

"OK, we go in hard." Weinberg's voice crackled over the walkie-talkie. "Denzel, you and Smithy stay back; let Martinez and me handle things. I don't have a lot of workable equipment left after someone – naming no names, *Smithy* – lost most of my guns, but we've got enough to take him out, then the spike will eventually take care of whatever's left."

"What about—"

"Last resort," said Weinberg, cutting him off. "Seriously, do not use that thing unless you have no other choice. I can't believe I even let you bring it."

Denzel adjusted the strap of the satchel he had slung across his chest. The contents felt heavy. He wasn't sure if he should find that reassuring or worrying. He settled on a bit of both.

"Got it," he said. "Stay out of your way; only use this if all else fails."

Martinez shot the bag a sideways glance, then turned his gaze to Denzel. "You know you're crazy, right?"

Denzel smiled. "Maybe."

"OK, picking him up dead ahead," said Weinberg. She

slowed, and Martinez waved his hand to stop the bubble. There was a *thonk* as Smithy crashed into it from behind.

"Sorry," he said, his face squished against the bubble like a short-sighted bird against a window pane. "My fault."

A blast of energy spat at them through the fog. Weinberg dodged sideways but the energy tore through Martinez's bubble.

Denzel experienced a worrying split-second of weightlessness again, before the bubble sealed itself.

"He's seen us!" said Weinberg.

"Oh, you think?" cried Martinez.

Weinberg's pack flared brightly. "Going in. Martinez, follow up with everything you've got. Let's do this!"

With a flash, she rocketed through the mist in the direction the shot had come from. Martinez took a deep breath, then gave a determined nod. He chanted something, made a gesture with his hands, then the bubble they were standing in became two. Denzel found his bubble slowing down as Martinez, now in his own sphere, pulled ahead.

"Hey! Where are you going?" Denzel demanded.

"Hang back here!" Martinez called, his voice sounding far away, and getting more so with every word. "We'll call you in if we need you!"

He disappeared into the mist, just as several flaring energy blasts illuminated it in a range of exciting colours.

Denzel rocked backwards and forwards, trying to propel the bubble on, but only succeeded in falling over.

Smithy caught up again. "All right?"

"They've gone into battle without us," Denzel pointed out.

"Oh. Right," said Smithy. He sniffed. "Is that a bad thing?"

"Yes!" said Denzel. He thought about this for a moment. "I mean... Well, I suppose they do know what they're doing. And we're just—"

"Loveable idiots."

"Trainees," said Denzel. He shuffled around so he was sitting on the bubble's curved bottom. "Maybe you're right. Maybe it's better if we do just hang back here and— Whooooaaa!"

The bubble rocketed forwards at alarming speed, throwing Denzel against the back wall. The Viking longship loomed into view just ahead. There seemed to be a *lot* of activity taking place on the deck. Magic sparkled, energy blasts crackled, and ... Denzel squinted. Something was coming towards him. Something bright and—

A flaming arrow tore through the bubble, popping it. Denzel's momentum carried him the rest of the way over the railing before he hit the floor of the ship with a *crunch*. He sat up, just as a skeleton swung at him with a rusty metal sword. Denzel kicked back and the blade embedded deep into the wooden deck.

Using both hands, the skeleton tried to pull the sword free. He was just giving it an extra-hard tug when Smithy slammed into him. The skeleton's arms stayed behind as Smithy and the rest of it went tumbling along the deck.

Just beyond them, Martinez and Weinberg were frantically battling a dozen more of the things.

"I thought you'd only call us if you needed us?" Denzel yelped.

"We need you!" Martinez replied.

As Denzel watched, several flapping white ghosts emerged from the fog, transforming into skeletal henchmen as they alighted on the ship. Martinez and Weinberg were surrounded, and for every one they took down, five more joined the fight.

"OK, not good," Denzel whispered.

A hand caught him by the back of the neck. This one didn't feel bony. Just the opposite, in fact. It was a hand made of solid muscle.

"Well now, what have we here?" boomed Ragnarok.

He hoisted Denzel into the air and pulled him close, so Denzel could see virtually nothing but yellow beard and yellower teeth. "I thought I took care of you earlier. You are a resourceful one."

"You d-don't know the half of it," said Denzel.

The Viking's mouth pulled into a sneer and Denzel was hoisted towards the ship's edge. "Wait!" Denzel yelped. "I brought you something. Treasure!"

Ragnarok hesitated. "Treasure? You mean loot?" He gestured around them. "I own your entire village. I have everything I want."

"No, you don't," said Denzel. He patted the bag. "You don't have this."

Rok's eyes narrowed behind his faceplate. "Show me."

Denzel glanced along the deck. Weinberg and Martinez were still holding their own, but only just. Smithy had pulled one of the legs off the skeleton he'd been fighting. He was chasing the skeleton round and round the mast with it. The skeleton, it turned out, was surprisingly good at hopping.

"OK, check it out," said Denzel. He reached into his bag. Ragnarok's eyes sparkled when Denzel pulled out an enormous red gemstone. A faint glow tossed and tumbled in the middle of it, as if the stone were somehow alive.

Or something inside it was.

"Well now," said Rok. "That *is* a fine treasure, indeed."

"I know, right?" said Denzel. "And you know what's great about it?"

"No. Pray tell, what might that be?"

With a jerk of one arm, Denzel knocked Rok's helmet off, letting the Viking's long blond hair tumble free, just as Denzel had hoped it would.

"It has a surprise inside!"

With a roar, Denzel threw the stone at the deck. He'd hoped it would shatter dramatically on impact, but instead it just sort of went *clunk* and lay still.

Denzel sighed. "Well, that's disappointing."

Ragnarok frowned. "Well, I'm sure I'll figure out the surprise in good time," he said. He took two big paces towards the edge, holding Denzel out in front of him. "Still, thank you for the loot. I shall very much enjoy—"

"Hey, Denzel."

Rok stopped and turned. Smithy stood holding the gem in one hand and a skeleton's leg bone in the other. With a flick of his wrist, he tossed the gem a metre or so into the air.

"Ready for that game of baseball?" he asked, then he swung with the leg bone.

Denzel watched it all unfold as if the world had

gone into slow motion just for his benefit. The gem reached the top of his flight, then began to tumble back down again. Smithy chewed his tongue in concentration as his borrowed leg bone came around in a wide, sweeping arc.

As the bone met the gem, there was a brief flash, a slightly less brief breaking noise, and then Denzel could see nothing but coarse, dark hair.

The longship lurched violently under the sudden weight of the monstrously huge gorilla that had suddenly materialised on the deck. King Kong looked around in surprise, then threw back his head and thudded his fists against his chest. The sound rolled like thunder across the skies, and the skeletons who had been attacking Weinberg and Martinez all scattered, becoming vapour again as they hurled themselves overboard.

"Odin's beard! What is that?" cried Ragnarok in a voice so sharp and sudden it caught even Kong's attention. The towering beast's head lowered. When it spotted the Viking standing before it, the fury on its face seemed to soften. The monster's eyes widened as it spotted Rok's head.

"That's Kongraueri, although we mostly just call him Kong for short," said Denzel. "And I should probably warn you – he *really* likes blond hair."

Kong's hand swiped at Ragnarok, snatching him up. Denzel tumbled free of the Viking's grip and rolled to a stop on the deck. He watched as Kong rubbed an enormous fingertip across the top of Rok's head, messing up the Viking's mane of yellow hair.

"Unhand me, beast!" Ragnarok raged, but his arms were pinned to his sides by giant gorilla fingers and no amount of squirming was going to break him free. "Release me, or face the wrath of Ragnarok."

"Hey, big guy!" said Weinberg, as Martinez waved his fingers in the air. He pulled his hands apart and the fog parted too, revealing a clear view of the Empire State Building and the shiny spike fixed to its roof. Weinberg smirked. "You know you want to."

With a screech, Kong launched himself off the ship. The force of the jump sent the longship into a spin, and by the time it had steadied, the monster was lost in the mist below.

"Where is he?" Denzel asked, peering down. "Where did he go?"

"Is that him?" asked Smithy, pointing to the upper floors of the Empire State Building, where an enormous gorilla was scaling the walls.

"Oh, yeah, that's probably him," said Denzel.

"He's going for it," Weinberg whispered. "I don't

believe it. He's actually going for it!"

"Come on," Martinez urged. "Just a little further."

The mist was drifting back in, but they could still clearly make out the shape of Kongraueri as he scrambled up the side of the building, just like he'd done all those years before. If Denzel strained his hearing, he could just make out Ragnarok's shouted demands to be set free. Kong, though, was having none of it. He'd lost his shiny-headed prize once before and seemed determined not to let that happen again.

With a clamber, a swing and a final leap, the beast's fingers wrapped around the spike. Lightning crackled from the pointed tip. A high-pitched whine screamed through the fog. Kong let out a low, guttural grunt of confusion and then he was gone, taking Ragnarok with him.

Weinberg whipped out a little handheld screen and hurriedly tapped it. She looked concerned for a moment, but then she threw her arms in the air and jumped up and down with delight. "Spectral Energy successfully crystallised!" she announced. "We got them both!"

Denzel and Smithy decided to get in on the jumping-up-and-down act too. They bounced on the spot, jiggling their arms in the air.

"We did it, we did it, we did it!" said Denzel.

"The famous 'use a famous giant movie monkey to catch an evil Viking ghost' technique," said Smithy. "Oldest trick in the book!"

"Uh, guys," said Martinez.

Something about the way he said it made everyone stop bouncing. They followed his gaze to the spike. Fog was swirling around it now, spiralling into a little tornado before being sucked into the tall metal prong.

"What is it?" asked Denzel. "What's wrong?"

"Uh, maybe nothing," said Martinez. "It's just..."

"It's draining the Spectral fog," said Weinberg. "It's sucking it all up."

"Of course!" said Martinez, slapping himself on the forehead. "It all makes sense. It's designed to be self-sustaining. It relies on Spectral Energy to power itself, that's why it stopped working in the first place, once the energy ran out. That's why the magic fixed it."

"And we just gave it a massive jumpstart," said Weinberg.

Denzel looked between them both. "Well, that's good, right? It'll get rid of all the fog and the ghosts and—" His eyes widened. "Oh, no!" he yelped.

"What?" asked Smithy. "Why's everyone looking at me like—"

Smithy was wrenched off his feet with such ferocity

that it made Denzel jump in fright. One moment he was there, the next he was hurtling through the churning fog.

And hurtling towards the spike.

CHAPTER 23

"Weinberg, Martinez! Do something!" Denzel cried.

Martinez raised his hands in Smithy's direction, but immediately lowered them again. "He's too far."

Denzel began to run. "Fine. He might be, but I'm not!" he said. Then, before Martinez could argue, he hurled himself over the edge of the ship, his arms stretched out in front of him like a superhero in flight.

He plummeted several metres, screaming, before Martinez managed to catch him. Denzel's stomach lurched as the fog became a blur around him. The wind tore at him, stealing his breath away. His eyes tried to close but he forced them open, blinking through the tears as he streaked across the sky after his friend.

"Hold on, Smithy!" he tried to shout, but the moment he opened his mouth the words were forced back down into his throat.

Smithy was a dozen metres ahead now, the spike just a dozen more beyond. He spun and flipped and rolled, the fog swirling around him as it was sucked in by the towering mast. Denzel could see the panic on his friend's face as he fought with everything he had to battle his way free of the spike's pull.

Denzel's hand caught Smithy's ankle and they both jerked to a sudden, eye-watering stop. Martinez was zipping through the air behind them in one of his flying bubbles, his fingers weaving whatever magic was holding Denzel in place.

The fog whistled past them. Limp white shapes flapped around like sheets drying on a washing line, before being consumed by the spike. Denzel tightened his grip as the pull on Smithy became even greater. The Spectral fog was making the spike even more powerful with every moment that passed.

"Turn it off!" Denzel cried.

"I ... can't. Too many ... protective incantations," hissed Martinez, and Denzel realised the spike was draining his magic too. It was taking everything he had just to keep them afloat.

The whistle became a roar around them, like pouring sand. Smithy twisted violently in Denzel's grip as the spike wrenched him away. Denzel made another grab for him but it was too late. Smithy hurtled, out of control, towards the spike.

He hit it with a loud *THWANG*, just as the roaring stopped.

Weinberg stepped out from behind the spike, holding two ends of a power cable. "It might have a lot of protection spells," she said. "But it's only got one power socket." One of the cables made a low *whumming* sound as she spun it around. "Gotta love technology."

Smithy pulled himself free of the spike. There was a perfect Smithy-shaped imprint on the side. "Hey," he said, turning to face the city. "Look!"

Denzel and the others turned. Well, technically Martinez turned Denzel, but the effect was much the same.

New York shone in the sunlight, the blue sky reflecting off its shining glass towers. The fog, the longship and everything else were gone. The city was a ghost-free zone once again.

Denzel glanced up at Smithy. Well, *almost*.

"They look happy, don't they," said Smithy, indicating

the thousands of faces lining the windows of the buildings below. They clapped and waved and cheered behind the glass.

Denzel noticed hundreds of people flooding out of the buildings on the streets.

Then he noticed how small they were.

Then he noticed that, without all that fog blocking the view, he was really very high up indeed, supported only by magic.

"P-p-put m-m—" was all he managed to say, but Martinez got the idea and gently lowered him on to the one-hundred-and-third floor beside Smithy and Weinberg.

Denzel immediately flattened himself against the wall and took several deep breaths. After a few seconds, though, he managed to force himself to approach the ledge and join the others in looking down.

The streets were filled with people jumping around, hugging one another, and dancing. From up here, they looked like ants. Thousands upon thousands of ants.

"Well, guys," said Denzel, looking from Martinez to Weinberg and back again. "I hope you have a *lot* of memory dust!"

Two days later, Denzel and Smithy stood outside the

airport security check, saying their goodbyes. Weinberg and Martinez were dressed in their respective uniforms but, in true New York fashion, no one batted an eyelid.

There hadn't been enough memory dust, not even close, but the Elders had promised "to intervene" and everyone had immediately stopped talking about King Kong, Vikings and giant octopuses (or octopi, depending on who you asked). Denzel had found that a little disconcerting but decided it was something to worry about later.

"So, six-hour flight, huh?" said Weinberg. "That sucks."

"Yeah. Pretty much," agreed Denzel.

"Still, was it worth it?" Weinberg asked. "Are you glad you came?"

"Uh … yeah," said Denzel, as diplomatically as he could. "It was certainly interesting."

"Please don't make us come back," said Smithy.

Martinez laughed. "What? But we never got that game of Battlefist."

"And it was you who asked to come visit in the first place!" said Weinberg.

"Ha. Yeah," said Denzel, then he frowned. "Wait, what? No, it wasn't. You asked us to come."

Weinberg glanced over to Martinez, then they both shook their head. "Nope," she said. "We got a message you wanted to come check the place out."

"We got a message you wanted to meet us," Denzel said.

Weinberg and Martinez both frowned. "Well, that's weird," Martinez said. "So that means ... what? Someone else wanted you to come here?"

"Why would someone want me to come here?" Denzel wondered.

"You opened the gate," Weinberg said. "When you touched it. It was you that made it open."

Denzel looked a little embarrassed. "OK, OK. But it wasn't on purpose! And we caught everything."

"We think," said Smithy.

Everyone turned to look at him. "What do you mean?" Denzel asked.

Smithy shrugged. "Well, we thought it was just the shark that came out to start with, but then there was a massive Viking ship and a big octopus. You probably noticed them."

"And we caught them, like I said."

"But how do we know something else didn't escape and make its getaway?" Smithy said. "You know, while we were distracted fighting sharks and Vikings and everything."

"So what are you saying?" Denzel asked. "That

someone deliberately arranged for me to come over here, and that they somehow knew I'd touch the gate and free whoever was trapped behind it?"

"Or *what*ever," said Smithy. "If there was enough room back there for a shark, a Viking ship, a huge octopus and, like, a zillion ghosts, I reckon pretty much anything could have been in there."

He grinned, then shook his head. "Although, when I say it out loud, it does sound pretty unlikely. Forget I said anything."

Martinez and Weinberg exchanged a glance. "Uh, yeah," Martinez said. "We'll look into it."

Weinberg pointed at Denzel. "You need to look into why you're a magnet for all this stuff," she said. "I know someone in the UK who might be able to help. I'll get the details sent to you."

"Thanks," said Denzel. He shifted uncomfortably on the spot. "You don't really think something else got out, do you?"

"Nah!" said Weinberg. "I mean ... probably not. I mean—"

Before they could discuss it any further, a pleasant female voice rang out. "Last call for passengers Denzel Edgar and ... er ... Smithy Smith. Your flight has finished boarding. Please proceed through security immediately."

"You better go," said Weinberg. Denzel opened his mouth to speak but she quickly jumped in. "We'll look into it. Now, go! You don't want to miss that six-hour flight."

"We do," said Denzel, as he and Smithy hurried towards the security check.

"Bye!" called Smithy. "Thanks for letting us play with your big monkey!"

He stopped when a large security man blocked his path. The guard glared at Smithy and Denzel in turn.

"Uh, 'big monkey' is a nickname," Denzel explained.

"For what?" the guard demanded as he checked their tickets and passports.

"For their... Um..."

"Magic horse," said Smithy. He blinked in surprise. Even he hadn't been expecting to come out with that.

"You played with their magic horse?" asked the man.

Denzel nodded slowly, not quite sure what else to do. "Yep," he said.

The guard eyeballed them both for several seconds, his hand resting on his holstered gun. Then, with a wave of his hand, he directed them towards the security gates. "Well, don't some people have all the luck," he said. There was a smile in his voice, even if his face wasn't showing it. "Have a good trip."

"Thanks," said Denzel, taking back his ticket and passport. "You too. Um, I mean... Have a good day."

The guard nodded, and this time he did smile. Denzel and Smithy scurried through the gate and, to their relief, neither of them bleeped.

"Oh, son," called the security man. Denzel turned and looked back at him. He was framed in the gate, all traces of the smile gone from his expression. His eyes were glassy, like a doll's, and his voice came out as a low, rumbling hiss.

"He is coming."

And then he stepped aside, and dozens of passengers flooded through the gate, bustling Denzel and Smithy towards their flight and whatever – or whoever – awaited them back home.

Have you read?

SPECTRE COLLECTORS

TOO GHOUL FOR SCHOOL

BARRY HUTCHISON

nosy crow

CHAPTER 1

Denzel Edgar was halfway through some particularly unpleasant maths homework when he saw the ghost.

He'd barely taken out his workbook when he first felt the icy tingle down his spine. He was sharpening his pencil when all the fine hairs on the back of his neck stood on end. Denzel looked around to find where the draught was coming from, but every window and door was shut tight.

He was wrestling with a head-wrecking bit of algebra when his eraser jumped out of his pencil case and flopped on to the dining room table. Denzel stopped writing and looked at the rectangular rubber with its graphite-stained ends. He looked at his pencil case. Then, with a shrug, he placed the eraser back inside.

A moment later, it hopped out again. This time, Denzel didn't move to return the rubber to the case. Instead, he just stared at it, wondering quietly what was going on. As he stared, his breath formed wispy white clouds in front of his face. It reminded him of being outside in December, only he was inside. And it was June.

Denzel's whole body began to shiver. He felt cold from the inside out, but he felt something even more troubling, too.

He felt like he was not alone.

"Wh-who's there?" he whispered. The words sounded smothered by the suffocating silence of the house. He heard nothing, saw nothing, but felt … something. A tickle of movement across his face and through his hair, as if the air itself were taking form around him, becoming something different, something more.

Down on the tabletop, Denzel's eraser stood on end. It walked towards him, rocking from side to side the way his dads would walk the wardrobe from one end of his bedroom to the other whenever they took it upon themselves to reorganise the place. Unlike the wardrobe, though, the rubber was walking all on its own.

Instinctively, Denzel slapped his hand down on the

waddling eraser. He felt it squirm in his grip as he forced it back into the pencil case and zipped it inside. The pencil case twitched and wriggled, so Denzel slammed his schoolbag down on top, and quickly backed away from the table.

He could feel his heart beating at the back of his throat. His dads wouldn't be home for another hour or more. He was all alone in the house.

So why couldn't he shake the feeling that he wasn't?

And then he saw it, reflected in the glass of a picture frame: a dark shape lingering in the corner of the dining room, spreading up the walls and across the ceiling like a nasty case of rot.

At first, Denzel tried to convince himself he'd imagined it. The dark thing behind him wasn't real. It couldn't be real. He was going mad, obviously. That last equation had fractured his poor overworked brain, making him see ... whatever that thing was.

He knew if he could just summon the courage to turn round he'd find nothing there but the empty wall. Maybe there'd be a shadow or something, but nothing like the writhing tangle of smoky black tendrils that was currently reflected back at him.

Slowly – ever so slowly – Denzel turned. As he did, he closed both his eyes, so by the time he was facing the corner, he was still none the wiser as to whether anything was actually there.

He wanted his eyes to open, but his eyes were having none of it. It took several deep breaths and a whispered pep talk before his right eye relented. His left one, however, remained fully committed to staying shut.

To Denzel's dismay, when he opened his eye he saw that the corner wasn't empty. The thing that lurked there looked like a cross between an octopus and a chimney fire. It was as black and intangible as smoke, with six or seven long tentacles all tangled in knots. The shape seemed to pulse in time with Denzel's crashing heartbeat, getting faster and faster as Denzel's panic bubbled up inside him.

One of the thing's tentacles reached out for him, and Denzel stumbled back. He raced for the door leading into the hall and pulled it open. The tentacle whipped past him, slamming the door again and holding it shut.

Denzel ducked and scanned the room, searching for something to defend himself with. The best he could find was a little plastic model of the Blackpool Tower that a neighbour had brought them back from holiday. It wasn't the ideal weapon with which to battle a malevolent supernatural entity, Denzel suspected, but it was the only one he had.

"S-stay back!" he said, thrusting the Blackpool Tower towards the smoke thing, pointy-end first. "I'm w-warning you."

One of the smoky tendrils lashed out. A snow globe – another holiday memento – exploded against the wall above Denzel, showering him in glass, glitter and a tiny reproduction of Edinburgh Castle.

Yelping in fright, Denzel covered his head, just as a dining chair flipped into the air and slammed down beside him with a *smash*. Denzel dived for the door again, but the tendril still had it held closed.

The window! It was Denzel's only chance of escape. Waving the Blackpool Tower in what he hoped was a vaguely threatening way, he leapt over the broken dining chair and raced towards the window. He was making a grab for the cord that would pull up the blinds when the whole thing exploded inwards, knocking him off his feet and on to the dining table.

Denzel's momentum carried him over the polished tabletop. As he slid off the other side, the table tipped, shielding him from the smoke thing – and whatever had blown his window to bits.

Cautiously, Denzel poked the top of his head above the table edge, just enough to give him a view of the room. Two figures stepped through the gap where the window and part of the wall used to be. It was hard to make them out through the cloud of plaster dust, but from their silhouettes it looked like the bigger of the two was carrying an assault rifle.

Denzel looked at the small plastic Blackpool Tower he'd somehow managed to keep hold of during his short flight across the room. After a moment's consideration, he quietly set it down on the floor.

"Scanning for hostile," barked the figure with the gun. It was a man, that was all Denzel could figure out. Young-ish, he thought, but he couldn't be sure. He jabbed his little finger in his ear, trying to clear out the ringing noise from the explosion. Someone must have heard the sound. Help would be on its way. With a bit of luck, no one would kill him before it arrived.

"Any sign?" asked the other figure. This one was a teenage girl, Denzel reckoned, and sounded far less confident than her partner.

"Can't pinpoint it," the man said, and something about his voice this time told Denzel he was a teenager, too. A red light blinked on the barrel of his gun, as he slowly circled on the spot. "But it's here."

Denzel glanced over to the corner. The black shape was still there, pulsing and twisting as before. He found himself gesturing towards it with his eyes, trying to draw the strangers' attention to it without being noticed himself.

"Perhaps the Third Eye of Sherm will shed some light on the situation!" the girl said grandly. Denzel heard the boy sigh as his partner began to mumble below her breath. The room was still one big cloud of white dust, but through the fog Denzel saw a shape illuminate in purple light on the girl's forehead. It was an oval with a circle in the middle, like a child's drawing of an eye.

"The Third Eye of Sherm!" boomed the girl, in a voice that rolled around the room. When the echo faded, the boy gave a disapproving tut.

"Do you have to do that every time?"

"Yes," said the girl. "It's tradition."

"It's dumb," the boy replied. "Besides, it blows our element of surprise."

The girl jabbed a thumb back towards the hole where the window had been. "Um... Hello? I'm not the one who obliterated the wall. The front door was literally five paces along the street."

"You have your traditions, I have mine," said the boy. "Whatever. Can you see it?"

"The Third Eye of Sherm sees all," said the girl.

"Yes, but does it see the hostile?"

The girl turned and scanned the room. The purple

MALPAS

glow of the eye on her forehead swept across the walls like a searchlight, passing right across the smoke-thing. "No," she admitted. "It doesn't see that. It can't be here."

The boy gave his gun a smack with the heel of his hand. The light flickered then came back on. "You sure? I'm definitely reading something."

"What do you trust more? Eight billion pounds of advanced tracking technology," began the girl. She tapped her forehead. "Or this baby?"

"Eight billion pounds of advanced tracking technology," said the boy, without hesitation.

Denzel wanted to scream to them that both the tracking technology and the fancy glowing eye were both rubbish, because the "hostile", as they called it, was right there in the corner of the room, just sort of hanging about looking ominous...